discovering KATE

discovering KATE

DIXIE OWENS

SWEETWATER BOOKS

An Imprint of Cedar Fort, Inc.
Springville, Utah

ISBN 13: 978-1-4621-2052-9

Published by Sweetwater Books, an imprint of Cedar Fort, Inc.
2373 W. 700 S., Springville, UT 84663
Distributed by Cedar Fort, Inc., www.cedarfort.com

LIBRARY OF CONGRESS CATALOGING-IN-PUBLICATION DATA

Names: Owens, Dixie, 1943- author.
Title: Discovering Kate / Dixie Owens.
Description: Springville, Utah : Sweetwater Books, an imprint of Cedar Fort, Inc., [2017] | Description based on print version record and CIP data provided by publisher; resource not viewed.
Identifiers: LCCN 2017017742 (print) | LCCN 2017026707 (ebook) | ISBN 9781462128075 (epub and moby) | ISBN 9781462120529 (perfect bound : alk. paper)
Subjects: LCSH: Organ donors--Fiction. | Brain--Transplantation--Patients--Fiction. | LCGFT: Novels. | Fantasy fiction. | Romance fiction.
Classification: LCC PS3615.W448 (ebook) | LCC PS3615.W448 D57 2010 (print) | DDC 813/.6--dc23
LC record available at https://lccn.loc.gov/2017017742

Cover design by Priscilla Chaves

Edited and typeset by Jessica Romrell

Printed in the United States of America

10 9 8 7 6 5 4 3 2 1

Printed on acid-free paper

Discovering Kate is dedicated to my good friend,
Gloria Powers, who taught me to give of self,
and to my wonderful husband, Howard.

Also by Dixie Owens

Becoming Kate

Prologue

Somehow, hidden in the back of her mind, Marcy Lindsay had always known that this day would come—the day when Kate Craig would find her way back into the circle of the Lindsay family. *Kate, the first and only brain transplant patient to survive the surgery.* But the donor brain now in Kate had belonged to a twenty-nine-year-old Elizabeth Ann Lindsay, or Liz, as she was called. Liz was the wife of Bruce Lindsay. Now Bruce was Marcy's husband.

Seated across from Bruce at breakfast that morning, Marcy listened as her husband read the article in today's paper, ". . . only person to survive brain transplant . . . performing at the September opening of the San Francisco Opera . . . was eleven years old when operated on . . . now, at age nineteen . . ."

Marcy knew that when Kate was only five years old she'd had spinal meningitis, followed by a series of seizures and, finally, a coma. Until the transplant, Kate had been brain-dead. Headlines from across the globe had celebrated the success of her recovery. But when the next three brain-transplant patients died shortly after surgery, the doctor who performed the surgeries left his practice. Outrage from those who thought the procedure was against the laws of God intervened, and no more surgeries were attempted again.

No one knew why Kate had lived while the others had not.

Except for me, Dr. Jamison, and Kate. Now she's back. What does she want?

Part I

Her Return

Chapter 1

A Ghost

As Marcy sat on the plaid blanket on the Golden Gate Concourse with her daughter, Adriana, and her step-daughter, Megan, she couldn't help but compare herself to the beautiful young woman who stood across the concourse onstage—Kate Craig.

Marcy was in her early forties, wore blue jeans, a red pullover tee, and dark sunglasses; nineteen-year-old Kate wore a green taffeta dress that showed off her cleavage. Shortly after the transplant, eleven-year-old Kate had been bald. Now her hair ran in lustrous ebony ringlets over her shoulders, whereas Marcy's dark brown hair was thinning and was styled in a simple pixie cut.

A cool September breeze washed over Marcy as she stared at the spectacle of Kate and thought about what this might mean to her family. Kate was a beautiful, talented young woman—not the strange little girl who had inherited Elizabeth Lindsay's brain and then moved away to study music seven years ago. When Liz died in a car crash eight years ago, Marcy had learned that Bruce had signed a confidentiality agreement, which meant that he didn't know what happened to Liz's body after it had been donated to science; fortunately, he had been spared the knowledge that his wife's brain now resided in Kate.

What would he think if he found out? Or if he knew that I was complicit?

Marcy didn't want to think about the implications of Bruce finding out that when she was Kate's physical therapist she had colluded with Kate to meet Bruce and Kate's children: Megan and Mark. She hadn't meant to fall in love with Bruce. She was just trying to help—to let Kate/Liz know how her family was coping with her "death" from a terrible car accident.

"Mom, where are you? You look as though you are a million miles away," Megan said.

That interruption brought Marcy back from her thoughts. She sighed. "Just remembering when I first met Kate. That's all."

"That is so rad," Adriana said. "That you were her physical therapist and now here we are to hear her and meet her after the performance."

As Marcy's two daughters chattered like two little mynah birds at her side, Marcy recalled those days following the surgery. Kate was supposed to have no memory of her former life, her data banks wiped clean. Only something had gone wrong. And now . . . Marcy closed her eyes, willing the memories gone.

When she opened them, she saw Bruce walking toward her, asthma medication in hand.

"Oh no!" Guilt and fear mingled as she saw her tall, handsome husband approaching her, his dark hair blowing from the afternoon sea breeze. Of all times, why had she forgotten her medication today? Fortunately, it wasn't much out of his way since he was taking their two sons to a ballgame.

Marcy hadn't worried about her relationship with Kate eight years ago. After all, Marcy was older, closer to Bruce's age, whereas Kate was a mere child back then. Marcy hadn't felt the need to compete. But Kate was no longer a child. She was a young adult. Marcy prayed that Kate wouldn't see Bruce, wouldn't want him back.

Now that she's so beautiful . . .

If there were a contest between this young, voluptuous singer and Marcy, she knew who would lose. She had no doubt about that, and that's what kept her up at night.

"Two minutes," the manager called from backstage.

Kate stiffened as the orchestra tuned up, feeling a combination of panic and exhilaration. She ran her hands from temple to crown, pushing her long, dark curls behind her ears.

"*Tesoro mio*, are you okay?" asked Giovanni Scala, the world-renowned tenor. As he touched her cheek, he pursed his lips, a question reflected in his dark eyes.

"It's nothing." Kate turned to him and faked a nervous smile. At any other time she would have enjoyed his attention—but not now. Not today.

He laughed and kissed her gently on the neck.

"Please don't, Gino," she said as she jerked herself away.

"*Cio e sbagliato*? What is wrong?" he asked, his face only inches from hers. "*Deo meo*, Kate, you look as though you have seen a . . . a . . ."

". . . a ghost," she whispered.

Gino gave Kate a puzzled look.

"I'm fine. It's n-nothing," she stammered. But she wasn't fine. Her heart was pounding and her ears were ringing. Worse, her insides were stirring like an old-fashioned butter churn. She ran her hand across her stomach and looked at Gino in an attempt to hide her qualms.

What would Gino think if he knew the truth? How would he react if he knew that Megan, her seventeen-year-old daughter from her former life, before the brain transplant, would be in the audience? The surgery was supposed to have wiped away Liz's memories. . . . Instead, her memories were that of Liz, wife to Bruce, and mother to Megan and Mark.

She choked back a nervous laugh.

"What is it? Why are you so anxious?" he asked.

"I don't know. Just a little stage fright, I guess."

"Not you," he said, looking at her candidly. "You are never like this."

"Maybe it's because this is the first time I've performed in a starring role in my hometown," she said.

"Look, Kate," he said, taking a paper from under his arm and thrusting it in front of her. "You have nothing to worry about."

"Brain Transplant Survivor Opera Star," the headlines in the *Chronicle* read.

Gino hovered over Kate, all five feet ten inches of him, as he read the story aloud, his cleft chin moving in a rhythmic cadence as he pointed to the lines: "Katherine 'Kate' Craig was branded a celebrity long before she could sing. YouTube videos have received over 800,000,000 hits of the young girl being wheeled out of Stanford Hospital."

She remembered that day. It seemed like a lifetime ago now, and yet here she was, facing her demons—or rather her past and all the memories that entailed, both good and bad.

"You see, you are loved here." He wrapped his muscular arms around her arms and waist. His green tunic felt satiny smooth against her skin. She shivered. "Come on, *mi amore*. This is your West Coast debut. You are a national . . . how do you say it . . . phenomena." He linked arms with her and patted her hand. "You can do this, my little songbird."

Kate wasn't so sure. Still anxious, she removed her arm and stepped away from him. She peered around the pavilion portico at the crowd, not caring that he seemed unhappy with her response.

"I'm going to continue warming up," he said, his voice less kind than before. "You may want to do the same."

"Sure," she said. "Soon."

Again, she scanned the audience. Hundreds of blankets and lowboy lawn chairs, jam-packed with opera lovers, filled the green. Lollipop shaped trees lined both sides of the beltway. She turned her head, eyes darting back and forth in desperate search of Marcy.

"Oh, God!" she gasped as she spied a woman on a blanket three rows back. Kate noticed that Marcy was still very attractive and thin, appearing even taller than her five feet and eleven inches.

Seated across from Marcy, and with their backs to the stage, two young women were rummaging through a picnic basket. One appeared to be willowy and sported long brown hair . . . *must be Marcy's daughter, Adriana.*

As the orchestra tuned their instruments, the two young women turned around to face the stage. Kate thought she was prepared for the sight of her daughter from her former life, yet when she saw Megan, she pressed her hand hard over her heart to keep it from leaping out of her chest.

My beautiful, beautiful baby.

She stared at the blossoming young woman who had inherited her—no, not her . . . *Elizabeth Lindsay's* straight strawberry blond hair and oval face. Although Megan sat cross-legged on the blanket, Kate knew by her long limbs that she was tall, like her father, Bruce. No one would ever guess that Megan had once been her daughter—Kate with dark hair, round face, and barely over five feet two inches tall.

We may look different, but I know how you feel. Oh, how I wish you knew me.

Her thoughts reeled back to Bruce, the man who had once been her husband, the man who had been her life, her best friend.

Where is he now?

Gino was gorgeous, but compared to Bruce . . .

I let go of Bruce seven years ago.

Was it fair to compare Gino to Bruce?

Kate forced her eyes away from Megan and studied Marcy, the woman who was now Megan's stepmother and Bruce's wife. Mixed feelings overwhelmed her—a muddle of love and envy. She ran her tongue up and down over the inside of her lower teeth, still startled at how different they felt from those in her former life.

Despite the jumble of feelings Kate had toward Marcy, she recalled the woman's strong but gentle hands in those days following the surgery. She could still almost feel the touch of the compassionate physical therapist. Marcy had helped her during the many months of her transplant recovery. For a time, Marcy had been her best friend, but her marriage to Kate's former husband and the loss of Kate's children had put a wedge between her and Marcy. Plus, although unspoken between them, now that Kate had become a woman, a woman who could possibly win Bruce back if she chose to, Marcy had begun to distance herself, so much so that their only communication these days was through email.

Determined to push these painful thoughts aside, Kate raised her hand to her right temple and felt the thin scar that rimmed her hairline from ear to ear. She unwillingly conjured up the image of Dr. Jamison, the famed neurosurgeon and Nobel Prize recipient who had performed the transplant surgery. Where was he now? What had become of him? Before Dr. Jamison had quit his practice, he had put her in the capable hands of a local doctor for her long-term care. Yet, despite her queries about her former neurosurgeon, her new doctor had remained quiet, telling her only that Dr. Jamison had asked for privacy since the surgery.

As Kate peeked around the edge of the curtain, her eyes reeled back to where Megan stood next to Marcy. The young girl's teal-blue eyes widened when she saw Kate. Megan flashed a smile, then waved at Kate and raised her cell phone for a photo shot. Kate felt a surge of pure joy. Her eyes welled up and a lump formed in her throat as she stared at her daughter, but disappointment soon consumed her as she realized that the girl's reactions were those of a fan, not a daughter.

Kate clutched at the Craig family keepsake pendant that hung from her neck and then turned away, almost tripping. Fortunately, her daughter hadn't seen the tears that were forming in her eyes as Kate ran an index finger under each eyelid to keep her mascara from smearing.

Today, after the opera, she could finally hug Megan . . . *my daughter.*

The very thought of this made her impatient to be finished with the concert.

The stage manager, who had been watching her from the wings, threw her a questioning glance. In response, Kate released a muted "mi, mi, mi, mi" and blew a stream of air through her lips replicating the sound of a small motorbike as she warmed up. She then reached for the water bottle, took a quick sip, swished it through her mouth, and swallowed. It was all a show. Inwardly she grieved for the lost years that separated her from her children—years when the close bonds of mother and daughter should have formed, years when her young son's voice would have been changing, years when the family would have decorated Christmas trees and celebrated holidays.

Kate practiced her deep breathing exercises and hummed to ease her tension. But how could she relax? Her friend, Marcy, and "was-band," Bruce, had wed a mere thirteen months and three days after her life as Liz ended. And now seventeen-year-old Megan and fifteen-year-old Mark called Marcy "Mom." Kate couldn't have picked a better mother for them. No, it was her fault. She had prodded Marcy into meeting Bruce. It had been her way of trying to keep track of her family. The outcome was perfect: a loving mother for her children and a good wife for Bruce.

Despite the warm summer day, Kate wrapped her arms tightly around herself. How many times had she blamed God and then asked His forgiveness for that careless moment eight years ago when her life as Liz had ended?

Once upon a time, she had been Elizabeth Ann Lindsay, a mom, a wife, and a returning college student. Now she was Katherine "Kate" Craig, a soprano, a graduate from the Juilliard School of Music, and one of the most sought-after names in the opera world.

Yet, deep down, she couldn't erase the fact that in her heart she would always be Megan's and Mark's mom.

"Eight years ago . . ." she whispered aloud.

She had been so caught up in the memories that she hadn't realized that Giovanni was once again at her side until he said, "*Cio*?"

"You're on," the stage manager cued.

Grateful for the interruption, Kate inhaled deeply, squared her shoulders and, hand-in-hand with Gino, walked onstage. She barely heard the sounds of applause and shouts of, "Kate, Gino, Kate, Gino, Kate . . ."

As always, she was well prepared for the arias, but how could she possibly prepare for a "friendship" with her daughter? And what about Mark and Bruce?

Yes, what about Bruce?

The orchestra music swelled. She expanded her diaphragm and opened her mouth, but the words caught in her throat as she saw a man walk out on the green. Kate suddenly felt dizzy. She would know Bruce anywhere. The man who thought she was dead. The man that—God help her—she still loved.

Chapter 2

Too Bizarre to Accept

Except for the false start, when Bruce had shown up with the asthma medicine, the performance was flawless. The tears dripping from Marcy's chin were as much from the thrill of having experienced beautiful music as the pain of knowing what she stood to lose if Kate were to want her family back. She didn't know if she could handle that. She only knew that she couldn't keep running and she couldn't keep Kate from her children. She owed her that.

Despite her fears, Marcy rose to her feet along with her daughters and added her voice to the "bravos" that were ringing out. Marcy had to admit she was mesmerized by Kate's voice. It was so youthful and clear while her presentation was mature, almost stately. Megan, who had been just as enthralled with Kate's singing, turned to speak to Marcy and frowned.

"What's wrong, Mom?" Megan asked. "Why are you crying?"

Marcy pulled a tissue from her purse and blew her nose. "Just . . . just so beautiful," she said as she fanned her face with the program in an attempt to hide her true feelings. Fortunately, Megan took her words at face value and smiled, clearly believing everything was okay.

The children must never know the truth.

"Come on, girls, let's fold the blanket and put these things in the car," Marcy said, pointing at the picnic basket and pillows. "We can come back in a few minutes, after the crowd has dwindled." She hoped the girls didn't detect the tremble in her voice as she added, "Then I'll introduce you to Kate, and you can get her autograph."

"Ah, that's tight!" Megan said.

Marcy affected a smile as Megan and Adriana jumped up and down and chattered as only teenage girls can do. She overheard a few words and phrases: ". . . just two years older than us . . . brain transplant . . . everyone loves her . . . I wish I could . . ."

"Whoa, Mom, look at all the people lining up to get her autograph. Will we have time to get one of our own or have a chance to talk with her?" Megan asked.

"Yes, yes, she knows we're here." Marcy glanced nervously at Kate who appeared radiant in her green gown.

Why do I feel guilty?

But she knew why. For seven years now, she'd been Mark and Megan's mother. She'd seen them through their illnesses, helped them with their homework, and kissed their scraped elbows while Kate had been forced to watch her children from the sidelines. Now, she wanted more access to her kids. Marcy had hoped Kate's memories would fade and, with time, she would move on and start a family of her own. Marcy had never suspected that the memories would become stronger, and that Kate would grow up to be a beautiful, talented young woman.

As Marcy was folding the blanket, she saw a momentary look of panic cross Kate's face—probably believing that they were about to pack up and leave. Despite her worry about what was to come, Marcy waved and hand-gestured that they would be back and then turned away. When she glanced again in the direction of the bandstand, she saw a middle-aged couple taking turns embracing Kate. Then a big, sturdy-built young man came up behind the singer. He walked with confidence and his brown hair, flecked with bits of amber, blew in the wind. His smile revealed a set of the whitest teeth Marcy had ever seen. Although it had been several years since she had seen them, she recognized the older couple as John and Donna Craig, Kate's parents. *The young man must be Kate's older brother, Josh.* She calculated his age. Josh was four years older than Kate. *So he's twenty-three.*

Marcy cocked her head and watched as Josh lifted Kate in the air and spun her around as though she were a weightless bird—Kate was so petite and Josh was so huge. They didn't look like brother and sister. How different they were now than after the surgery. Josh had been so angry, had felt neglected with all his parents' attentions focused on Kate. They had clearly resolved those issues from the look of things.

She was surprised to see Giovanni Scalia walk over and tap Josh on the shoulder. As he did so, Josh released Kate and the handsome tenor took her by the hand and gently guided her into an intimate embrace.

Marcy felt a momentary wave of relief. *Thank god, she has a boyfriend.* Perhaps she was wrong about Kate's intentions.

Relieved, Marcy whistled as she walked toward her car.

Adriana pulled at her mother's sleeve and squealed, "Mom, you're killin' it. I can't believe you know Kate!"

Marcy gave her daughter a squeeze.

Girl, you have no idea.

Bruce and his sons, Mark and Shaun, rose from their stadium seats and raised their arms above their heads. Scarcely had Bruce finished yawning when the boys yawned too.

"Seventh inning. Time for a hot dog and a Coke," Mark said, his hair tasseled in the warm breeze. Like Bruce, his oldest son's hair had turned from his boyhood blond to dark, curly brown. He was only two inches shorter than Bruce. *And still growing.*

Bruce raised an eyebrow as he recalled the pictures he'd found of himself when he was fifteen and how much his son looked like him at that age—except Mark had his mother's eyes.

His mother.

Why hadn't Marcy remembered her inhaler and meds? He hadn't been ready to see Kate. To think that maybe Liz was . . . *no I can't go there.* Kate simply couldn't have Liz's brain. He had signed a confidentiality agreement, so although he knew Liz's organs had gone to science, he had no idea if they had been used in any transplants. It was ridiculous to speculate, and the odds of Liz being Kate's donor had to be infinitesimal. Still, Liz *had* died at nearly the same time as the first brain-transplant procedure and in nearly the same area. He pinched his lips together in a pout.

Six-year-old Shaun punched his right hand into his mitt, reminding Bruce that he needed to focus on the kids. "Hey, Dad, can I have a hot dog? And how about some curly garlic fries and a Coke?"

"You're hungry, huh?" he said, relieved to be thinking about someone other than Kate as he ruffled his young son's hair. "Okay, Coke for you two." He felt like he needed a beer after tonight . . . after seeing Kate for the first time in years, but he opted for a cola instead.

For the next ten minutes, he feigned interest in conversations with his sons, but his mind was racing. Although he loved the Giants, today the diversion of the ballgame wasn't working very well. He couldn't shake his uneasiness about his wife and daughters meeting Kate.

"Can I have popcorn, too?" Mark asked.

"Sure," Bruce mumbled as he reached for his wallet and checked his cash.

His mind unwillingly raced backward. For almost a year after Liz's death he'd been clueless about the extent of her organ donation . . . or perhaps he hadn't wanted to know. But on Independence Day, almost a year following her tragic accident, he heard twelve-year-old Kate sing at the college stadium. Although Liz had never been much of a singer, she had loved music, especially opera, and had always wished she could sing. The song Kate sang that day was one of Liz's favorites. Plus the three earlier "run-ins" with the girl had left him wondering. But for the last seven years, he'd pushed his suspicions deep into his subconscious.

According to media reports, Kate had left the Bay Area to attend a private music school. After graduation, she had been accepted on scholarship to Juilliard.

The cliché fit, "Out of sight, out of mind." Denial. That's where his mind had gone. The thought that this girl, Kate, might have Liz's brain and memories was just too bizarre to accept. *But now she's back and my wife and daughters are at her concert.*

He rotated his head, heard it creak, then readjusted his sunglasses back onto the bridge of his nose. Had Marcy known all along about Kate and deceived him?

You're being ridiculous, he told himself. But was he?

"At least it's a close game," Mark said. "Four to three, Giants ahead and it's been a good hitting game. Maybe they'll win the series again this year!"

Bruce nodded absentmindedly.

"Hey, Dad, what time do you think Mom and the girls will be home?" Shaun asked.

"What?" he said looking down at his son's eager face. "Ah . . . probably around five," he replied as he reached the counter.

"Three hot dogs, a large popcorn, a medium curly garlic fries, and three large cokes," he said to the vendor.

"Who would rather go to a stupid old opera than watch the Giants play?" Mark asked, eyes wide in jest.

"Beats me," Bruce said.

"Yeah, beats me too," Shaun mimicked.

"That'll be forty-nine dollars," the vendor said.

Bruce pushed the cash back into his wallet and handed the man his credit card.

Chapter 3

That's Just the Ticket

As Marcy and her daughters walked toward Kate, she heard Kate say to Gino, "Those are my friends. I don't want them to wait in line for autographs."

"As you wish," he said. "Your friends are my friends."

Kate apologized to her fans. "I'll be right back," she said, then rose from the autograph table and hurried toward the trio.

Marcy could see the anticipation in Kate's eyes. She knew that Kate had seen Bruce and that it momentarily stopped the show. Maybe forgetting her meds had been one of those Freudian slips. Maybe she wanted to see their reaction.

Now that Kate had become a woman, no longer a child, a subtle shift had taken place between them. A barrier had risen. Marcy couldn't blame Kate for the change in their relationship. After all, how would she have reacted if the roles were reversed? At this point, she was keenly aware that Kate undoubtedly wanted to see her children. As a mother, Marcy understood that. When she and her first husband separated, her daughter, Adriana, became the center of her life. She knew from Kate's shared emails and Facebook correspondence that Kate had followed the lives of Megan and Mark from a distance. Now that distance was gone.

Megan ran toward the portico and was the first to reach Kate's side. "Can we get your autograph? And Giovanni's too?" she asked, talking a mile a minute. "Can we also take selfies with you?" She extended a pad and a pen toward Kate while clutching a smart phone.

Moments later, Adriana appeared at Megan's side and Marcy soon joined them.

Marcy held her breath as she watched Kate stand no more than an arms-length from her one-time daughter. Kate licked her dry lips and a smile broke out on her porcelain face. Still, she offered a wide grin to the threesome and said, "Of course. Better yet, come with me to the bandstand and we'll sign one of the promotional pictures."

Kate guided them to the front of the line, reached under the table, and pulled up a folder, retrieving two photos. She signed them, "To my BFFs, Marcy, Megan, and Adriana—Much love, Katherine 'Kate' Craig." She handed them to Gino to sign. Marcy could see that Kate's hands were shaking.

As soon as Gino autographed them, Kate stood and motioned to her brother. "Oh, Josh, will you take photos, pictures of Gino and me with Marcy and then with each of the girls?"

Marcy felt her heart beating faster.

Pictures with her daughter.

"We'll email copies to you," Kate said. Marcy could hear a subtle break in Kate's voice and saw that she was holding back tears of joy.

Kate's brother, Josh, approached, camera in hand. "Stand over there, in front of that tree." He motioned to Marcy, Gino, and Kate.

Although Marcy seemed reluctant to join in, she did as asked. Kate placed a tentative arm around Marcy's waist while Gino stood behind them. Despite the fact that Marcy was tall and considered pretty for her age, she felt homely next to Kate.

"Thank you for keeping in touch with me all these years, especially for sending me pictures over Facebook," she whispered in Marcy's ear, neck outstretched.

"Smile," Josh said.

Marcy positioned herself and smiled. *Click.*

"Now turn a little, and you and Marcy look at each other."

Kate tilted her head to look into her friend's eyes. *Click*.

"Now you," Kate said as she pirouetted away from Marcy and crooked her finger in a come-over-here gesture to Adriana.

The girl grinned and walked over to Kate and Gino's side.

Marcy noticed Gino giving Adriana a flirty grin and she saw Kate elbow him in the ribs. He gave out a shocked "Ah!"

"Gino, you stand on this side of me so that there's more sun on Adriana's face." Kate glared at him, and although he moved over, his jaw was clenched tight.

"Say cheese," Josh said.

Kate smiled and Marcy saw that Adriana lifted an eyebrow and offered the camera a flirty smile . . . or was it meant for Josh? Click.

Marcy chewed on her lip. Things were getting complicated.

"Now your turn, Megan," Kate said, hand extended toward her daughter. The palms of Marcy's hands suddenly went damp.

Megan giggled. "This is so sick."

Gino kept his place, and Kate moved her arm around her Megan. It was obvious to Marcy that that moment was a little piece of heaven for Kate. *Click*.

Kate sucked in her bottom lip and released it with a pop. "I have a surprise. I want your family to be my guests at the 100th Annual Opera Gala and opening night performance of *La Traviata* this coming Friday night."

With that pronouncement, Kate turned and waved at her manager. "Cassie, please do me a favor. Give Marcy the envelope with the invitation."

Kate grinned at Marcy. "Let's see, you'll need six, isn't that right? Three of you, and then there's your husband, Bruce, and your sons, Mark and Shaun."

Her manager trotted over and gave Marcy the engraved invitation and tickets.

"Compliments of Miss Craig," Cassandra said.

"I've always wanted to repay your kindness," Kate said. "I hope this goes some small way toward saying thank you for all you've done for me."

While Marcy's lips moved silently as though trying to speak, Megan and Adriana squealed with delight.

Gino winked at Megan. "How nice. Your family and friends will be at the party." He made a gesture, bowing deeply and brought Megan's hand to his lips.

"That's enough!" Kate said.

Clearly oblivious to Kate and Marcy's brief exchange, Megan squealed, "We're gonna party! I feel just like Cinderella."

Josh moved forward. "We know who's *not* your Prince Charming," he said, giving Megan a toothy smile. He then stared icily at Gino.

"She is a pretty little thing, isn't she?" Gino said.

Marcy squared her shoulders. "That's all quite wonderful. But I doubt that the male members of our family will be interested."

Touché.

"Why not?" Kate asked.

"They're not interested in opera. They're avid sports fans," Marcy said, her eyes darting toward the exit, making it clear that although she had agreed to today's visit, she wasn't ready for anything more, and especially where Bruce was concerned.

To be fair, Kate had only to see the girls' reactions to know Marcy wasn't lying.

"Please," she pleaded. "Tell them it would mean a lot to me. I'm sure they'll have fun. I'll make sure that they do."

"I'll try, but I doubt that I'll be successful." Then, as if to add salt to the wound she added, "I guess you don't know how my husband and boys feel about classical music. It's way out of their league."

Chapter 4

A Cup of Tea Would Be Nice

Melbourne, Australia

Dr. Donald Jamison worked the wet clay, trying to form the likeness of his beautiful Russian wife, Inna. It was his fourth attempt. But regardless of his efforts, the face he always found staring back at him in the reddish-brown clay was Kate's—a twelve-year-old Kate who he hadn't seen in more than seven years. Her round face and short dark curls were forever chiseled in his mind along with the beautiful songs she sang at that Independence Day celebration.

His shoulders slumped, a strand of his thinning gray hair falling across one eye as he pushed the bust away at arm's length. Although he felt safe here on the other side of the world, he couldn't escape the memories of that girl. She walked through his nightmares and her face appeared whenever he heard a soprano sing or the mention of a surgery.

His small cadre of friends in Melbourne knew he was a retired doctor, but they didn't know that he was a Nobel Prize recipient—the world-famous brain-transplant surgeon. Kate was his first human brain-transplant patient . . . and the only one of four to survive.

"Can I get you anything?" Inna asked, her voice holding only a trace of her Russian accent, as she spun into the bedroom-turned-art-studio. Her bright pink slacks and tunic and the lilt in her voice gave his spirits a passing lift.

"A cup of tea would be nice," he said. "I'll wash up and join you in the living room."

"Oh, darling, that's beautiful," she said as she walked over to him, bent over, and studied the clay bust. "Who is it?"

"You know very well who it is. It's her again . . . doesn't matter what I try to do, it comes out Kate."

Inna shook her head. "Well I don't think it looks like her pictures, but I have news that will take your mind off her." She placed a warm hand on his shoulder. "New neighbors are moving into the flat across the way. I just met Alice and Thomas Burnett and their son, Noah."

"Oh? It'll be nice to have another youngster in the neighborhood."

"Well, he's not exactly a kid. Noah's a young man, twenty-six years old, to be exact . . . and in a wheelchair. From my brief conversation I had with him, I'd say that he's quite eloquent, very smart. But the poor man . . . well . . ." She paused and turned on the faucet to wash out the studio sink.

"Well, what?"

"Mentally I'd say he's quite healthy, but physically—I really don't know. I'm not the doctor in the family," she said, one eyebrow lifted. "But he did ask if either of us liked to play chess. He says he's pretty good. I told him that you're the chess player in the family, so I think you may have a new challenger."

"Oh, he likes the game of kings? Well, maybe I can give him a run for his money," he said as he pulled the bust back toward him and pinched a thin line around the rim of the bust's head. Then he squashed the clay flat and mumbled something under his breath.

Noah Burnett laughed as he dropped his razor to the floor for the second time in five minutes. "Twenty-six years old and ya can't perform even the simplest of tasks," he said to the emaciated person he had become, a person he barely recognized in the mirror. "Ah, well." He set the razor down. He would ask his mother to help him later.

He wheeled himself into the living room where his short, sweet mother, slightly overweight and wearing a flowered dress and an apron, had a protein shake waiting for him that he could sip through a straw. Just one more hurdle he'd had to jump, upon learning that he had cystic fibrosis. At first he'd been angry, but over time anger had soon given way to acceptance. Lately, to keep his mother from crying, he'd learned to incorporate humor into their lives. That had made all the difference in the world.

"Take a look at this, Darl," she said, handing him yet another science magazine with a twist on his condition. He'd read everything from herbal remedies to the latest high-tech cures, but most of them came with the proviso that the breakthroughs could occur within the next fifteen years. He didn't have that long. He would be lucky to survive the year.

Fortunately, his disease hadn't stopped him from working from his computer or using his still-sharp mind to play chess. If he'd had the physical ability or stamina, he would be playing on the chess tours, but that was impossible now.

"So what have we got today, Mum? Eye of newt, or have we moved on to mushrooms and toadstools?" he said with a mischievous grin to which she clouted him one, gently of course.

"Just read it. Yer a smart fella. If anyone can find a solution to yer illness, it'll be you."

He rolled his eyes in jest. He wished he had as much faith in himself as his mother had in him. Intelligence could only get him so far with the limited time he had left to find the remedy—if there was one—to the disease that was day by day sapping his strength so that he spent many afternoons napping.

"Well, son, yer not going to find the answer with that attitude!" She ruffled his hair, which had become less shiny. His skin had become more sallow and his cheekbones more pronounced.

"Yes, yes, I'm on it, Mum." He held up a pretend sword and held it out to her. "But I have to be knighted proper like if ya expect me to slay *this* dragon," he said, "so go on. Knight me."

"You've been playin' too much chess, Sweet. I think it's gone to yer head." But all the same, she held the pretend sword and laid it one by one on each shoulder to which he bowed from his wheelchair. "Okay, now drink up yer shake, Noah," she said, chiding him, all the while smiling.

"That's *Sir* Noah to you, Mum."

"Well, Sir Noah, yer not too old to take over my knee," she said, lifting her eyebrows to let him know she meant business.

"Okay, okay!" he said, throwing up his hands. "I'm on it. And I'll find us that cure. After all, I have a reputation to uphold now that I'm a knight." With that, he took a sip of his shake, all the while wishing it were a meat pie instead.

CHAPTER 5

PARTY TIME

Seconds after Bruce heard the automatic garage door open, his daughters skipped into the family room, Adriana waving a photo and Megan sing-songing, "We're going to a party!"

"Look, Dad," Megan chirped. "We got Giovanni Scalia and Katherine Craig's photo, and they both signed it."

The family dog, Algae, came running into the room carrying a bright yellow ball in his mouth. He chomped on it, causing it to make loud squeaking noises. Then he jumped on Adriana and dropped the ball at her feet, demanding that she play fetch with him.

"Not now," Adriana said as she pushed the ten-year-old mongrel away.

Algae picked up the ball and carried it over to Bruce, dropping it at his feet.

"And we got an engraved invitation to go to the annual opera and the gala afterwards. It's this Friday! And we have box seats," Megan said, still wide-eyed from the day's adventure.

At the thought of seeing Kate again, Bruce felt as though he couldn't breathe. As he reached down to pick up the ball, he slopped

V8 juice onto his shoes. The thick stuff wet one leg of his jeans and puddled over the floor.

He cursed when he saw the puddle. It would likely stain.

Algae, with tail tucked between his legs, retreated through the dog door.

"The invitation is for the whole family. Isn't that wonderful?" Adriana said.

Mark, who was gazing into the refrigerator and within earshot, growled, "Big whoopdie doo. I'm not goin' to no stupid opera."

"Me neither," muttered Shaun without ever taking his eyes off his video game. "It's just a bunch of women screeching. Yuck."

As Bruce mopped up the juice with a rag he'd retrieved from the kitchen, he glanced up in time to see Marcy trudging through the doorway, head down and arms filled with picnic paraphernalia. Her face was ashen. She glanced at Bruce and then slowly cast her eyes downward again.

"Help your mother," Bruce said as he relieved Marcy of the basket. "Don't leave her to bring everything inside. What's the matter with you two anyway?" He cursed himself and his bad mood. Usually, he was easygoing, but today had undone him. Seeing Kate, he couldn't help but wonder . . .

Determined not to let his worries get the best of him, he stood to help Marcy, who sighed and plopped her keys and purse on the countertop. The odor of overripe fruit and cold chicken quickly permeated the room.

"Oh, sorry, Mom. We'll go get the rest," Adriana said, nudging Megan.

Megan nodded and said, "Yeah, no problem, Mom."

As soon as the girls exited the room, Bruce walked over to the kitchen counter and picked up the promotional photo of a young Kate with a dashing young man holding her in a dramatic pose. Bruce's eyes moved from the couple to the signature, *Much love, Katherine "Kate" Craig*. He studied the small *e*s in both the names "Katherine" and "Kate" and flinched when he noted that they were written like small capital *e*s, just the way Elizabeth used to make hers.

He placed the photo on the counter, walked to the refrigerator, and took out another V8, then quickly set it back on the glass shelf, still trying to wrap his head around the idea that Kate might have Liz's transplanted brain. He grabbed a Coke instead. It would take stain remover to get the V8 juice out of the carpet. Hopefully, he'd have better luck with the Coke.

"So?" Marcy asked tentatively.

"Opera's not my thing," he said as he popped the top of the cold pop and raised the can to his lips.

Was that relief he saw wash through her? And if so, why? What was she hiding? He loved Marcy, but he needed time to figure things out. To come to grips with the almost eerie similarity of the handwriting. He knew he should talk to Marcy about what he had found, but first he needed to get his emotions in check, to process what he had learned, and to come to some sort of decision. Until then, he feared he would be no good for anyone.

With that, he grabbed some carpet cleaner from under the sink and the rag and then finished sopping up the juice on the family room floor. Afterwards, he walked to the laundry room, threw the rag in the washer, and slammed the lid.

I think Liz is back.

Chapter 6

Gino

A knock on her hotel room door plucked Kate from her memories. Except for the fact that some members of the Lindsay family might not come, the day had been more than she had hoped. She peered through the peephole to see Gino's face smiling back at her, then opened the door just enough to talk directly to him.

"You're early," she said. "I thought we weren't leaving for dinner until 7:30."

"Yes, but I thought maybe we could visit for a while." Gino rested his hand against the doorjamb, not moving.

"Another time," she countered, hoping he would take the hint.

"Why not now?" he said, as he gently pushed on the door.

Kate pushed back. Although most of the time she enjoyed Gino's company, she was aware of his reputation, but most of all, she was determined to guard her *own* reputation. She wasn't about to risk doing something that could end up in the tabloids.

"Come back at 7:30 and we'll have dinner together then."

He shook his head, a glint of steel in his dark brown eyes. "Look, I promise to be a gentleman."

Kate sighed. "Gino, my dear *gentleman*, come back at 7:30 and not a minute earlier."

She closed the door and locked it.

At nineteen years old, when she was still Elizabeth Lindsay, she had become pregnant and married Bruce. Despite everything, she didn't regret her folly back then or she would never have given birth to Megan. And there was no way she would ever consider Megan a mistake. Part of her missed the old life, the closeness, being needed and loved. Most of all loved.

Opera had given her a second chance to have a career, to use her head. She just hadn't counted on how lonely it would be on the road, traveling from hotel room to hotel room. She missed the intimacy of a mate, the fulfillment of a family. She thought about Gino, the one constant in her life. Sure, she had desires. But this time she understood hormones. Besides, Gino wasn't what she considered "marriage material." And she wasn't ready to move on and to start another family.

I already have one.

Chapter 7

Like a Cancer

Marcy excused herself from the table and instructed the girls to do their late-night snack dishes. Then she retreated to the bedroom, stepped into her walk-in closet, kicked off her shoes, and removed every stitch of clothing. For several moments she stood there naked, feeling lost. She ran her hand over her neck in an attempt to smooth out any new wrinkles. Then she bent over, picked up her loafers, and placed them neatly on the shoe rack. She grabbed her discarded clothing and stuffed them into the hamper—to get rid of the smell, the dirt.

Kate was like a cancer. For seven years Marcy and Kate had had only minimal contact—email, Facebook, the occasional card. In the meantime, Marcy had stepped into her new life just as Kate had stepped out. And Marcy had been happy—deliriously happy. She had thought all was well, but now Kate (or was it Liz?) was back. And she wasn't the same gawky little girl as before. Now she was . . . perfect.

Oh God, make Liz go away.

The passage of years and her own deceitfulness weighed her down. *Why did she tell me her secrets eight years ago? Why didn't I run from that hospital room when I had the chance? Why didn't I tell Dr. Jamison about the botched memory-removal procedure in the beginning?*

Marcy placed her arms across her chest. What if? She knew now that if the memory removal had been successful, Kate would have died—just as the next three transplant patients had. But back then no one had known that memory was a vital part of a brain-transplant patient's survival. And today, only she and Dr. Jamison had that awful knowledge. The one and only successful surgery hadn't been a *brain* transplant. It had been a *body* transplant.

The Craig family had noticed the personality shifts but thought it was part of the reintegration process. What they hadn't expected was her wide command of the language and her newfound talent as a singer. As for Kate, she had done her best to act the part of a young teen, fearing that if they knew about the memories, they would want no part of this woman who was no longer their daughter. And what man could reconcile with the fact that his wife was in an eleven-year-old body? It had been a nightmare . . . for Kate *and* for Marcy. So, for better or worse, they had stayed silent. Now they were paying for that silence.

Marcy fingered the lightweight cotton nightie on the closet hook, but opted for the long flannel gown hanging next to it. She slipped it over her head. It was still summer and warm, but she was shivering. She needed comfort, and she doubted she would get any from Bruce tonight.

Chapter 8

The Main Event

Bruce checked the sleeve length of his rented tuxedo as he parked the Chevy SUV in a self-parking lot at Opera Plaza, just two blocks from the Opera House and City Hall. He still couldn't remember how he'd been talked into this. Oh right, the girls. They had wheedled and begged and eventually cried. Now, here he was.

He glanced at his wife. The fragrance of Coco Mademoiselle by Chanel, the perfume he'd given her for her last birthday, drifted through the car. She wore the same blue brocade dress and dyed-to-match shoes she had worn the day they had married. He knew that she had other cocktail dresses, just as nice, if not nicer. But he knew why she chose that outfit—as a reminder.

"You have the tickets?" he asked Marcy.

She snapped opened her silver clutch and held them up. "Everything's right here."

"Well, then let's do this," he said, trying to maintain his composure.

Megan opened the back passenger door and stepped out into the parking lot. "This rocks," she said as she smoothed her black faux-diamond-studded mini dress. Then she reached back and retrieved the black-and-white hand-painted silk shawl that her girlfriend let her borrow for the occasion. Her long rhinestone earrings made her seem grown up. Bruce wasn't ready for his daughters to become women. It was happening too fast.

Adriana climbed out the other side and slipped the small gold purse with the long chain over her head, whipped it across her body, and placed it by the hip of her off-the-shoulder, too short, practically see-through dress. Bruce had objected to it, but Marcy told him it was "in fashion" and to "let it rest."

At least the boys were safe at home—he hoped.

As part of the pre-opera events, City Hall was awash in red lights giving the structure a dusk-like glow. Hundreds of people were milling about and entering the historic building prior to the evening festivities at the Opera House where the main event would be taking place later.

Marcy's heels clicked as she walked. Dah-dun, dah-dun, dah-dun, dah-dun. It was like she was saying something and he should know the language by now, but he didn't.

"What is that?" Megan asked, pointing at the main entrance.

"I think it's a scaled down replica of the Arc de Triomphe, a Paris landmark," Marcy explained. "I guess because the opera is set in Paris the designers put in this special entrance."

"Sparing no expense, I'm sure," Bruce said as he jingled the keys in the pocket of his rented tux.

As they entered the building, he stopped to stare. It was magnificent. The Doric columns, bas-relief sculptures, and marble floor were all palatial.

As they walked through the grand foyer, Marcy linked her arm with his in a very deliberate fashion that hinted of ownership. As she did, her faux-diamond bracelet caught on her brocade dress and snagged a long thread causing her to gasp. Just as she seemed to gather herself, her foot gave way. If it hadn't been for Bruce's arm, she would have tumbled headfirst.

"Are you okay, Babe?" he asked as he helped prop her back up. He noted a look of despair as she moved her foot back and forth. She gave him a weak smile.

"I'm fine," she said with little conviction. Then she let go of his arm, turned toward the girls, and drew the invitation out of her clutch. She stared at the beautifully embossed page.

"It says cocktail reception at 5:00, so you two can have a soda or a virgin whatever. Then we sit down to a lavish Parisian themed dinner at 6:00." She looked up from the invite and added, "I'm sure we'll have arranged seating so you'd better wait to find out where we'll be before you two take off on your own. The opera starts at 8:00, which means we need to leave City Hall no later than 7:45. Afterward . . ."

"We party!" Megan chimed.

At the second floor, they entered the spacious Rotunda. Again Bruce had to stop and gawk at the majesty of the building.

"OMG," Adriana blurted.

"May I see your reservations?" asked one of the tuxedoed workers faking a French accent.

Marcy handed him the card. "Oh, yes, Madame, this way please. You are a special guest of Mademoiselle Craig. You and your family will be seated at the front with the Craig family."

For a moment, Bruce panicked. The idea of sitting with Kate and her family terrified him, and he broke out into an instant sweat. As they followed the usher, a waiter walked by with a tray of champagne. Bruce reached out and took one. He managed a long gulp before coming up for air as he trailed the usher to the Craig table. To Bruce's immense relief, he discovered it was empty. He let go a deep sigh and a not-too-indiscreet burp to which Marcy narrowed her eyes at him in warning.

To his chagrin, the table was set for ten.

Megan and Adriana looked at each other and grinned.

"I think we'll go check things out," Adriana said.

Megan twirled in a half skip and said, "Yeah, we're chillin'."

"Be back before 6:00," Marcy said. Then they were gone.

Bruce lost count of the hundreds of opera patrons who were parading about displaying designer gowns, accessories, and nineteenth-century tuxes. Some were successful in capturing the styles of the *La Traviata* period—floor-length gowns, loads of lace, and lots of cleavage. But maybe the champagne was causing the illusion.

He motioned to a barman.

"Could you order me a flute of champagne too?" Marcy asked with just a hint of an edge.

"Oh of course, sorry. What would you like?" he asked, brow furrowed.

"I'll have the same as you . . . *Sweetheart*," she added with a not-so-subtle hint of possessiveness.

After the drinks were delivered, Marcy sipped hers in silence. When the flute was half empty Bruce noted that she sat up as straight as a flagpole as a middle-aged couple and young man were being led in their direction.

"Who are they?" Bruce whispered.

"Huh? Oh, Kate's parents and brother."

Bruce scooted his chair back and stood. So did Marcy.

"Marcy, it's so good to see you again," the woman said. She walked over and gave Marcy a hug.

Marcy turned. "Bruce, this is Donna and John Craig, Kate's parents."

Bruce gave an acknowledging nod to Kate's mother, a small woman with close-cropped hair, then extended his hand to the tall man with dishwater-blond hair that was graying at the temples. "Nice to meet you," he said.

"And this strapping young man is Kate's brother, Josh," Kate's father said.

"How do you do, sir?" the young man said. Bruce noted that Josh was a good two to three inches taller than him and probably outweighed him by forty pounds—every bit solid muscle. The young man's tuxedo shirt seemed a bit ill-fitted across his massive chest.

Once they finished introductions, Josh seated his mother and Bruce quickly pulled out a chair for Marcy. John sat next to his wife, which was directly across the table from Bruce.

"You're a very lucky man, Bruce. You have no idea how much Marcy meant to Kate's survival. Your wife is a very caring and compassionate woman."

A very caring person. Bruce had always thought so, and yet he was having a hard time wrapping his head around the fact that

Marcy may have deceived him. Had she known Liz was alive, in some form or fashion, and never told him? If so, she had stepped into Liz's shoes and never looked back, and he had been none the wiser. His throat constricted at the thought.

Bruce knew that he and Marcy couldn't skirt the issue much longer, but he wasn't sure how to broach the subject. All he knew was that he had to talk to her soon. He fiddled with his cufflink and watched it fall to the floor. He felt his face warm as he reached under the table to retrieve it.

To his dismay, when he returned to the table, the awkward conversation continued. Bruce tried to keep track of questions and to give sensible answers, but he kept staring at the place settings. He could see Megan's and Adriana's, and the two set aside for Mark and Shaun. Next to John was an empty one. He couldn't see the nameplate, so he decided to ask.

"I see a place setting next to you, John. Will Kate be joining us?"

"Oh, no. That place is for my mother. She should be arriving any moment now. Kate eats very little before a performance. And there's so much preparation: costumes, warm-ups, getting into character. But she'll join us for the party afterward."

"You can count on that," said Kate's mother, Donna.

Bruce could see by Marcy's expression that she felt equally uncomfortable, and he immediately felt sorry for her. This had to be as hard on her as it was on him. He squeezed her hand wondering why he had come. What had he hoped to achieve?

She gave him a wan smile, clearly grateful for his support.

Five minutes before six o'clock, Adriana, Megan, and a very stately Mrs. Kelly made their ways to the table. Introductions were made and soon after, dinner was served.

With any fear of seeing Kate for the next half hour gone, Bruce relaxed, the smell of garlic drifting through the hall. Even Marcy seemed less tense now, Bruce noticed, as scores of tuxedoed waiters, all with their hair parted in the middle, scurried to deliver French-themed delicacies to their assigned tables.

"Dad, I read that one of San Francisco's top chefs put together tonight's menu," Megan said. "I've never had anything French . . . except maybe French fries."

Josh, who had been silent until now, said, "Hey, that's my favorite food!"

As the meal was delivered, the waiter explained each dish: escargot with garlic and parsley butter, Gruyère cheese Gougeres, salade Nicoise, soupe au pistou, eggplant Provencal, steak au poivre. Each course was paired with an appropriate wine by a very French-looking sommelier who explained the nuances of the divine liquid. The girls were served sparkling apple juice or the soda of their choice. Bruce wasn't big on snails, but add a little garlic and butter to anything and he could tolerate it.

He watched the girls pick through the dishes, pushing items back and forth over their plates—apparently not sure if some were truly edible. At first this made him smile—until he saw certain looks passing between Megan and Josh. The two had been seated next to each other. Megan's eyelashes fluttered every time Josh said something to her.

Regardless of the two glasses of champagne that he'd downed, Bruce knew he needed to sober up quickly. Their daughter was growing up right before his eyes, and if he wasn't careful she might soon be dating Kate's brother.

Chapter 9

Lovely Seventeen-Year-Old

The orchestra played music from opera scenes while the scent of chocolate, pecans, and honey hung in the air over the after party, but despite all this, Bruce couldn't stop fidgeting. He glanced toward the entrance. Kate should be here any moment.

Bruce, Marcy, and the two girls had been seated in one of the coveted box seats for the opera. He had been unnerved when Kate looked directly at him when she sang Violetta's mournful aria—the one the character sang while leaving her lover to protect him from ruin.

Why did you look at me?

Although Bruce hadn't understood the Italian words, he had seen the English translation of the opera flashed on the screen above the stage. He clearly knew what she was singing because he had been staring at her throughout the aria. Was it love, concern, or disdain that he felt? Probably all three. He tried to calculate what might happen now at the "after party." Would she spend much time with them or would the crowd take her attention?

What do I care? I don't know, but I do.

From the distance, he could hear her green satin gown make a rustling sound as she bobbed a petite curtsy in respect for the officials who had just come up to greet her. The deep green gown complemented her fair complexion and long, dark hair that was now piled high atop her head with a crescendo of curls trailing in back.

"Lovely party. We always enjoy the galas. And tonight's opening performance was truly superb," one of her tuxedoed male admirers said, his wife nodding in agreement.

And he watched as Gino, who was surrounded by his own circle of admirers, left them and strutted over to Kate's side.

Kate saw Bruce and his family mingling in the crowd. Bruce was as trim as ever, his hair still dark and curly except for a few white wisps at his temples. Her heart stilled at the sight of him. He was as handsome as she remembered him to be.

Her head felt woozy as she twisted the gaudy bauble on her finger, recalling the plain gold wedding band she had once worn. Although it had been seven years since she had seen Bruce, the sight of him was unsettling. During that period, she had gone through the physical teenage angst all over again, yet this time with the insight of an adult, knowing that things would get better over time. To counter all the conflicting emotions, she had poured herself into music, one of her great loves as the adult Liz. Only now she had the voice to make her dreams of singing possible. It had been the one saving grace during those tumultuous years. Now, seeing her family again, all the needs and wants for a family that she'd had as Liz returned in a great torrent of emotion.

"I'm so sorry," Kate said to Gino and the old woman, heat rushing to her cheeks. "Would you please excuse me? I see some dear friends arriving."

"Pardon me, too," Gino said, rushing to join Kate who had already made a beeline toward Bruce and the kids. "What are you doing?" he hissed as he caught up with her. "You just walk away from some of our biggest supporters? It's not . . . professional."

"Um-m-m," Kate said, unable to focus on Gino just now, her thoughts still on her old life, a life she'd thought she had finally put in the past . . . until now.

Gino's eyes trailed Kate's. "Oh, I see, it's those people . . . the ones from the park. What makes them so special that you would be rude to such important people?"

"I wasn't rude. I met with them." She tried to give him a look that said go away, but he remained at her side—glued despite the many admirers trying to stop and talk with them.

Kate's heart played a staccato in her chest as she forced herself to walk, head high, shoulders back. *Don't run.*

Marcy held her breath as Kate approached them.

"I'm so happy you and your family could make it," Kate said, trying to sound lighthearted and carefree. "Did you enjoy the dinner and the opera?"

"Just lovely," Marcy said through pale lips. Then she turned to Bruce. "I don't think you've met my husband."

Marcy purposefully emphasized the words "my husband." She saw Kate blanch.

"It's such a pleasure to meet you. I've heard a lot about you," Kate said as she reached out to shake Bruce's hand.

For several seconds Bruce didn't say anything, just gazed at her, his mouth parted ever so slightly. He wet his bottom lip with his tongue. "I've heard a lot about you." He took her hand and gently raised it to his lips, a gesture he had done often when he and Liz had been married.

Marcy felt as though her soul had just shriveled. She saw moisture gather at the corners of his eyes, and for a moment she thought he would take Kate in his arms. Time seemed to stand still, everyone and everything around her was slipping away.

Gino tapped Kate on the shoulder. "Cara, you forgot to introduce me," he said as he wrapped his left arm possessively around Kate's waist.

Marcy felt her face go red with anger. She stood beside Bruce and stared at Kate until Kate quietly pulled her hand away.

"Mr. Lindsay, this is Giovanni Scalia, the world-renowned tenor," Kate said.

Bruce and Gino shook hands, but it looked to Marcy more like a standoff after an arm-wrestling match.

Kate didn't know what else to say. Hadn't she been the one to thrust Marcy and Bruce together in the first place in an attempt to become closer to her family, to reconnect in some small way? But she hadn't counted on growing into a woman's body, hadn't forgotten what it was to need a man, children, and a family. God help her, she missed it. The days and months on the road feeling lonely and tetherless had reminded her of all she missed. It had become an aching, cloying need that had festered inside her until she'd been able to stand it no more.

But now, Marcy looked as upset as Kate felt. Shame burnished her cheeks. *What have I done?* The girls shifted their feet back and forth as though uncertain what exactly was happening.

Thank god for Megan, who, even as a small child, could read her family's moods and diffuse the tensest of situations. She twirled in a half skip and said to Gino, "I don't know why everyone is acting so weird. As for me, I feel like a princess. And this place looks just like the grand ballroom in the first act of the opera."

"You *are* a princess," Gino said throwing out his arms as if to encompass the palatial space. "This ballroom was modeled after the ones in Roma, Venice, and Vienna."

"Really?" she asked.

"Really," he said with a twinkle in his eye. "So, what did you think of the opera?"

"It was such a sad, romantic story," Adriana said, clearly taken up by the aria.

"I know, it was sad," Megan agreed, then quickly rebounded adding, "but I hope we can do this again. Wouldn't that be great?"

Kate glanced at Bruce and saw that his face was flushed and that something akin to anger had replaced whatever brief exchange they'd had together when he'd kissed her hand. Her early fantasies about tonight of reconnecting with her family were quickly fading into the cold reality of the evening. What had she expected? To waltz back into everyone's life, to become Mrs. Lindsay again, to simply shove Marcy aside? At the very least, she had hoped it would be a chance to see and enjoy her children, but instead, it was obvious that Marcy was angry and Bruce . . . well, Bruce was *Bruce.*

Bruce was relieved for the momentary hiatus as the two girls gushed about their evening at the opera, and yet he could almost feel the waves of heat radiating off Marcy even now. She had tried to be cordial, but any attempt at friendliness had all but evaporated the more the evening lingered. At this point, all he wanted was to get this evening over with as fast as possible.

Just then, from a side wing, Josh rushed over and tapped Megan on the shoulder. "Did I hear you love the opera?" he asked.

"I do, and wasn't Kate amazing?" Megan said, clearly starstruck.

"I know, my sister's really something, isn't she?" Josh agreed, the pride evident in his voice.

As Bruce listened to them banter back and forth, he realized he didn't know what to think about Kate. On the one hand, he was astonished by her accomplishments. She'd become a beautiful young lady. And it was clear by her actions that this was the "Liz" he had always known. But he couldn't get over the fact that both Marcy and Kate had deceived him. Both had known the truth, and yet they had let him mourn, had stood back as he had wallowed in despair and said nothing. How could he forgive either one of them for that?

"Kate's something, don't you agree?" Megan said, taking Bruce's hand and peering up at him, waiting for an answer.

"You bet she is," he said, trying to avoid both Kate's and Marcy's eyes. "She's . . . really something."

As if to remind him where his loyalties lie, Marcy slipped her arm through Bruce's arm, pulled it tight to her side, and sent a silent message with her body language: *she* was Mrs. Lindsay, and no one, living or dead, would get in her way.

"I can't thank you enough for inviting us," Marcy told Kate as she practically pulled Bruce forward, still arm-in-arm. "Your generosity is overwhelming. I can guarantee you that if we'd had to pay for a night like this, we would have had to hawk our house and *our* kids."

Once again Marcy had made it clear to Bruce that she was both wife to him and mother to their children. He didn't know whether to feel annoyed or pleased by her actions. More than anything, he felt numb. His wife had lied to him, and this plagued him.

"I'm so sorry that Mark and Shaun wouldn't come. But boys will be boys. Isn't that right, Bruce?"

Bruce bit back his frustration at the situation, his eyes trained on Kate, who was staring just as intently at him. If only he could talk to her, understand why she had lived a lie all this time.

"Bruce, isn't that right?" Marcy repeated.

Unnerved, Bruce merely nodded and looked away.

When he finally turned back, he noticed Kate blinking rapidly. Like Bruce, she had obviously read the message loud and clear. Marcy was asserting her ownership of him. But how could she possibly think that a nineteen-year-old woman, Liz's brain or not, could simply walk into their lives and start up where she had left off? He peered at Marcy, trying to view the situation as she must. A beautiful young woman, in the prime of her life and the fantasy of many a young man, was attempting to reconnect with her husband. If the shoe had been on the other foot, and Marcy were being pursued by a handsome young man, Bruce knew how he would feel. He would have decked the guy.

Still confused and frustrated, Bruce was about to allow himself to be led away, but just then an orchestra began playing in the background and the ballroom floor began to fill with dancers.

Josh stepped forward, put a hand out, and said, "Megan, would you like to learn how to waltz? I can teach you. I learned it in school a couple of years ago."

Megan flashed a wide-eyed grin and took the young man's hand. Before anyone could say another word, the two were on the dance floor, Megan stepping on the young man's feet as they skirted the dance floor. It soon became clear to Bruce that the eyes of the young couple were glued to each other in a way that spelled trouble.

Kate's brother . . . our daughter . . . I won't allow it.

Marcy must have had the same impression because her eyes narrowed as she whirled and rushed toward the dancing duo. Bruce caught his wife by the arm before she could cause more of a scene than she had already.

"Let's dance," he said in a growl that caused those nearby to turn and frown. They walked onto the floor, leaving Kate behind. At that moment another young man asked Adriana to dance.

Bruce maneuvered Marcy and himself closer and closer to Josh and Megan, then intentionally bumped into Josh.

"I'll take over from here" he said, propelling Marcy toward Josh as he commandeered Megan and led her in a ridiculous two-step away from Josh.

This night was going from bad to worse.

It wasn't supposed to be this way. What was Josh thinking? Her brother was a great guy, and Megan would be lucky to have him. She trusted him implicitly, and yet it was unnerving to see the two together.

As Kate pondered what to do next, she felt a warm breath on her neck and a soft brush against her arm.

"Ah, *mi amore*," Giovanni said as he ran his index finger across her wrist. "Where have you been? I turned and you were gone. Look here," he said, as a handsome, spectacled Asian-American man with a lovely woman at his side came toward them. "The mayor of San Francisco and his wife would like to meet you."

Despite the interplay taking place between Bruce and Josh, Kate did her best to acknowledge the pair.

"This is Mayor and Mrs. Li," Giovanni said, his eyebrows uplifted in a plea for her attentiveness.

Kate made quick work of introductions, her eyes still tracking her family's every move.

"My wife and I would like to welcome you to our city."

"What a lovely performance," the woman said. "You two make such a perfect couple." She winked, causing Kate's face to flush with warmth.

Despite the innuendo and the pride Gino seemed to take in her words, Kate merely said, "You are too kind."

At another time, meeting such notables would have delighted her, but Gino's attention was not entirely welcome. After all, he had a reputation with women, and although he had told her it was merely his way of building a following by playing the lothario, she wasn't so sure. She hoped that Mrs. Li's words hadn't given him the wrong impression, because right now she wanted—no *needed*—to be with her family. They came first.

She tried to be polite to the honorable mayor and his wife, but she couldn't keep from glancing at the spectacle of Marcy and Bruce trying to keep Josh and Megan apart. It was like watching an old pirate movie as Josh made a bold swashbuckler's leap to Megan's side, whispered something in her ear, and then took Megan's arm and moved toward the dessert table.

Oh, no! Kate raised her hand to her mouth and tried unsuccessfully to stifle a gasp. Her brother, no matter how much she loved him, could not date her daughter. Or could he? It *would* be one way of getting to see more of Megan, after all. And at least with Josh she would know Megan was in safe hands.

"What is it, Kate?" Gino asked, a deep frown marring his perfect features.

"Excuse me. I'm so sorry, Mayor and Mrs. Li, but I'm afraid my brother is about to cause a scene."

Her shoes tapped a rhythm in time with the orchestral music. With each new step she felt more power, more justification, and more determination. As the crowd parted she saw the two with plates in hand helping themselves to the pastries and truffles on the dessert trays. At each stop, they took turns whispering something into the other person's ear.

Kate quickly located Bruce and Marcy, who stood at the far end of the table staring at Megan and Josh. Even from a distance, Kate could see the blood pounding at Bruce's temples as he and Marcy exchanged angry words.

"Oh, there you are!" Kate said as she purposely maneuvered between the young couple. "What are you two up to?" she asked with one eyebrow raised.

The pair merely chuckled. She had to get them apart before Bruce and Marcy imploded, and Kate's dreams along with it.

"Josh, I was hoping you would ask me to dance. Besides, you should give this lovely seventeen-year-old girl a chance to dance with the other young boys here," she said, hoping he would get the picture that Marcy and Bruce were none too keen on the age difference, though she had been just as young when she had married Bruce.

"Cool it, Sis," Josh said, not taking the hint. "Megan is almost eighteen and she has just agreed to go out with me next Sunday afternoon."

"If my parents say that it's okay," Megan said with a dimpled smile, her eyes staring up into Josh's. "But I think they'll give their permission."

Kate tried to contain her worry as she turned to Josh. "Have you checked this out with Mom and Dad?" she said, throwing a glance Marcy and Bruce's way in hopes that Josh would catch on that not everyone would be happy with a budding relationship between them.

Josh gave her a questioning frown. "What's with you, Sis?" he asked. "Mom and Dad would never have a problem with it."

"No, no, you're right," Kate said, quickly amending her words. "They will love Megan."

Still, Josh was her brother, and Kate was Megan's mother. Besides, Marcy and Bruce would never go for such a friendship, which was evident by the glares they were throwing her way.

She closed her eyes to will away the confusion. How could she ever explain all of this to Josh, or Megan, for that matter? With renewed determination, she opened her eyes. She would leave it up to Marcy and Bruce. For now, it was enough that she might be able to see her daughter again on a regular basis, *if* everything worked out between the pair and *if* Marcy and Bruce gave their blessing . . . and that was a big *if.* If not, well . . . she would cross that bridge when she came to it. But how to get Marcy and Bruce's okay? If anyone could sway their decision, Megan could.

She couldn't help but smile at the thought of welcoming Megan into her home. This could be the opportunity she'd been waiting for to turn things around. Maybe she could even become friends with her daughter if she could win her over. Suddenly both hope and music seemed to fill the air.

"Actually, I think it's a wonderful idea." She grinned at the two and tried to maintain decorum even though inside she wanted to laugh, dance, and shout hallelujah.

Clearly Marcy felt threatened by any question of Kate having a relationship with Bruce, but Josh could very well bring Megan to her side.

At that moment, Bruce and Marcy appeared to announce that it was time for them to leave. Adriana pouted, but picked up her purse. Megan whispered something in Josh's ear and then giggled and joined her parents.

"I'd be happy to walk you to your car," Josh said to Megan.

"That won't be necessary," Bruce said, and then he grabbed Megan's elbow and steered her away.

Chapter 10

Fun for a Day

The next morning, Bruce was still reeling from meeting Kate the night before. He and Marcy hadn't spoken about the evening, their feelings still too raw, but now, like it or not, they would have to deal with the repercussions, because Megan wasn't going to let them off the hook.

"Why can't I go?" Megan demanded, as she stared down at him where he sat on the patio in one of two Adirondack chairs, her face shadowed, backlit by the sun.

He wagged his finger in his daughter's face. "Josh is an adult and you're a minor, still in high school. We don't want you going out with him. Do you understand?"

Marcy stood next to Megan, arms akimbo nodding in agreement with her husband. She raised a hand from her hip and bit at a callus built up next to a fingernail, a bad habit she often fell into when she was nervous.

Megan's nostrils flared. Bruce knew to brace himself when she got like this. "What is with you two? It's not like we're getting married or having sex. His parents will be there, and it's just a stupid swim party and barbeque. Besides, what's with the age thing? You started dating my mother when she was about my age, and you two were the same age difference as me and Josh."

"That's irrelevant," Bruce said between clenched teeth, but felt the sting all the same, because, of course, she was right. Who was he to talk? He decided to try a different ploy. "Look, the truth is we need you to babysit Shaun. Both Adriana and Mark have practice sessions at church today as you well know."

"Not a problem. I have money saved. I'll pay Patty to babysit. She says she's available," Megan quipped, her eyes steely.

She could be so stubborn, Bruce realized with a sigh. *Like her old man.* "It has nothing to do with money. We don't trust Patty. Besides, Shaun is only six and he likes you to babysit him."

Megan stomped her foot. "Since when? You've used Patty twice before and thought she was good. And why can't one of you take Shaun with you? He might learn something. He might even do more than sit around the house playing video games all day."

Bruce wove his fingers together and raised them to his chin. He felt beat. Conflicted. *She looks just like Liz.* Josh was no doubt a good kid, but he was still a young man with raging hormones. But that wasn't the half of it. What really bothered him was that he was Kate's brother. And what if Kate *did* have Liz's brain, which he suspected even more now than he had before meeting her at the opera? Would she want Megan back? Would she want *him* back? This was all just too confusing.

"A little soccer or karate would be good for Shaun. If he doesn't get some exercise he may become one of those kids with childhood diabetes." Megan smiled a sassy smile and raised her brows. "I'm just thinking of his welfare."

Bruce dug his hands into his pockets and shook his head. "And what do you hope to gain from this 'relationship'?" he asked.

Megan cocked her head as though mulling over his question. "Fun for a day. That's all . . . and maybe a chance to get to know Kate. She's awesome. And I think she likes me."

Bruce groaned. That was the last thing he wanted to hear. How could he get through to his daughter?

"You really don't have a good reason for telling me no," Megan said, her iron-straightened hair whipping around her face as she spoke. "My homework is up-to-date. My chores are done. His parents will pick me up and drive me home. So what's the big deal?" she asked as she patted Algae's head.

The dog licked her hand.

"Go inside and let me talk with your mom," Bruce said.

Megan rolled her eyes and stomped into the family room. Her flip-flops made a snapping sound as she departed. Algae followed like a shadow.

When Megan slammed the screen door behind her, Marcy turned to him and asked, "What are you thinking? You're not going to let her go, are you?"

Bruce held out his arms, palms up. "Darn it, Marcy, you're as much to blame for this situation as anyone." He hadn't meant to sound so harsh. "You think I don't know the game you've been playing? Why did you keep in touch with Kate all these years? Why didn't you tell me the truth? I *know* who she is."

Marcy gasped and let out a brief sob, but Bruce was too angry to go to her just yet. Instead, he rolled his shoulders to get relief from the mounting stress.

"Megan's right. I can't stop her from going. I give up."

Bruce stood and walked to the screen door, slamming it behind him.

Chapter 11

Wheels Turning

Melbourne, Australia

Jamison stood motionless, shoulders slumped, and stared at the gray door. He raised his fisted hand to knock and then withdrew. He lowered his head, fear chastising him. Ever since the brain surgeries at Stanford and the deaths of those three patients, he found it difficult to be around people with health issues. It was a reminder of his deficiencies as a doctor. A reminder that he had been foolish to play God. Worst of all, their deaths had been a reminder that he was human. Too human.

Only Kate had survived.

Since then, he had left his practice and moved as far away as possible to put the past behind him. Now Inna was trying to force him to engage the world again—to face his fears.

Again, he reached out to knock, but in the end flinched and turned away. How many nights had he awakened in cold sweats recalling each of his patients' faces? How many funerals had he attended? His therapist had called it PTSD, and he had to admit, that's what it felt like. Anxiety had become his constant companion. He took one step from the portal, then stopped and stood still as though he were staring into Medusa's eyes. He blinked and clamped his teeth so tightly that his jaw muscles quivered.

Then he had an epiphany. *I've woven my world entirely around Inna.* Yes, they had walked through the Melbourne parks and attended the flag-waving Veterans' Day parades. *But I chose to move us halfway around the world to be as far away from Stanford Hospital as possible.*

He had been so proud and pompous back then. Now, he felt as good as dead.

"No, I'm not!" he hissed.

He spun, squared his shoulders, and rang the bell.

The sound of soft footsteps increased as someone neared the door. A red-headed, middle-aged woman with an apron tied about her waist opened the door.

"Can I help ya?" she asked.

"I thought I should introduce myself. I'm your neighbor, Donald Jamison. I think you've met my wife." He felt his face warm.

"Ah, g'day Mr. Jamison. I'm so glad you came by. My name is Alice Burnett."

Jamison returned a cautious grin to the woman with the fading red hair and the Aussie singsong lilt. He noted that she was a good foot shorter than him and nearly as wide as she was tall. But she had a glint in her eye that revealed inner strength.

"Please, just call me Donald," he said as the fear fell from his shoulders.

"My husband is out right now. He should be back in a jiff, just a jaunt to the Woolies for some fresh fruit. But please come in and meet our son, Noah," she said as she motioned him into the flat.

"I hear he likes to play chess," Jamison said.

"Aye, indeed he does. Thinks himself a champion—plays on the Internet, but much prefers to look his rivals in the eye."

Alice walked toward the hallway and said in a loud voice, "Noah, come here. We have a visitor."

Jamison noted that the room was set up for a wheelchair user—no fluffy rugs and good, wide hallways and aisles. Additionally, useful items were at easy reach for one in a wheelchair.

"Can I offer ya a cuppa?" Alice asked.

"Yes, that would be very nice," he said as he heard a door make a high-pitched squeak.

The noise of wheels turning across the hardwood floors announced Noah's arrival.

"Noah, this is Dr. Jamison from across the hall. He's come to meet you and take you up on your challenge to a game of chess."

"Please, just call me Donald," Jamison said.

"G'day, sir. Pleasure to meet ya." Noah extended a hand in greeting. "Oh, and Mum, I'll take a cuppa too."

Jamison shook the young man's hand and noticed that he showed some strength and manliness in his grip, but with some trembling evident in his palm. "It's nice to meet you, too, Noah."

The young man was gaunt but nonetheless sat board-straight, and his eyes showed a determination that Jamison hadn't seen since medical school. His pale blue shirt and jeans hung loose on him as though he'd lost a good deal of weight since they'd been purchased—or perhaps they had just been hand-me-downs from some bigger brother.

"Do ya take any sugar or lemon in your tea?" Alice asked.

"Oh, no, just plain," he said.

"So, Dr. Jamison, I hear ya play a mean game o' chess," Noah said as he wheeled up to a table.

Jamison pursed his lips. "Used to. It's been a while. But at one time I was considered pretty darned good . . . if I must say so myself."

"Well, you two have fun," Alice said while placing cups of tea on the table. "Cheers! I have some chores to tend to in the other room, so I'll leave you to your pleasure." She glanced at her son with a sadness born only by parents of seriously ill children. Then she turned, scurried down the hallway, and disappeared into one of the rooms.

Jamison observed that the chess table was already set up to play. In spite of the young man's disease-ravaged body, he displayed a playful grin that made Jamison feel instantly better. Perhaps Inna was right. This might be just what he needed to boost his confidence.

"Your move, Doctor. You're white."

As Jamison shuffled to his flat, he felt much older than his years. A weight seemed to settle on his shoulders—double—triple gravity pulling at him.

He walked into the living room and looked at the buds growing on the plants on the sill—early harbingers of spring. Usually spring was his favorite time of the year, but knowing the fate of his newfound friend threw ice on these signs of hope.

He walked through the house but didn't see Inna. She wasn't in either the kitchen or the bedroom, so he looked in her office and saw that she was at her computer.

"How was your game?" Inna asked.

"I lost," he said with a pout.

"Well, I'm sorry you lost, but you needn't take it so hard. It's just a game," she said.

"It's not 'just a game.' It's strategy. It's thinking beyond the moment. It's a brain twister." He screwed up his mouth. "But losing is not the reason for my attitude."

Inna, looking crisp as usual in a pale gray turtleneck and black, cotton slacks, stopped staring at her screen, pressed a button on the side, and closed the device. "So tell me," she said. "Didn't you like Noah?"

"I like him very much. He's not only a genius, he's sincere and . . ."

"And what?"

"He's dying. His body is withering away—incurable—cystic fibrosis. I doubt he'll have a year left in him."

"Oh, how awful. He seems like such a sweet young man too. His parents must be devastated."

Jamison rubbed his jaw. "He had such dreams too. Wanted to be a doctor, like me, he said. Such a waste. Such an awful waste."

"I guess the best we can do is to be understanding—give him some pleasure in his remaining months," Inna said. "Why not let him win again?"

"Let him? He can do that without my help," Jamison said as he sat down in his recliner with a plunk and lowered his clean-shaven chin to his breastbone. He sat like that for some time, thinking. What could he possibly do to help the boy? After a long pause, the idea finally came to him in a flash of insight. He jerked his head up, widened his eyes, and snapped his fingers.

Chapter 12

He Loves Me, He Loves Me Not

Marcy lay ever so still, wondering how to talk to her husband. He was on the other side of the bed, not touching her. Their king-size bed had never felt this big.

I saw how he looked at her and how she looked at him.

She felt a lump welling up from the center of her breastbone to the back of her throat. She didn't want to cry. She just wanted straight answers from the man she loved.

But what if he says he wants her? God help me. What will I do?

"Bruce, are you awake?" she asked as she touched his shoulder.

"Hmmm." He turned over and faced her, but still kept his distance. "We need to talk. You haven't spoken civilly to me since the picnic at the park."

"I can't imagine why." Anger masked the hurt in his eyes.

She sat up and turned on the bedside lamp. "Oh, Lord, well, I know why. And that's why we have to talk. This stomping around, huffing and puffing when you walk by, it's driving me crazy. Yes, Kate has Elizabeth's brain. And yes, she remembers her life before the surgery. Every detail. There. I've said it." She frowned, struggling to hold back her tears.

Bruce stared at her with a look of disgust crossing his otherwise handsome features. "Everything between you and me has been a lie. You didn't meet Liz at the opera in the park; she wasn't your email buddy; you didn't come to my house to bring condolences to your *friend's* family. You snuck into our lives clothed in one lie after another. Why did you do it? What did you hope to gain?" His features were dark, almost foreboding. For the first time in her marriage, she felt afraid of him.

Marcy felt the lump growing in her throat, hurt to the core. "Bruce, please don't hate me," she said with a sob, tears cascading down her face. "I was trying to help her . . . Kate—Liz, whoever she was. She wanted to know that you, Mark, and Megan were alright. She *begged* me to come. She even made up the storyline. I didn't want to fall in love with you. It just happened. I—I'm so sorry."

He sat up so suddenly that she flinched. "So, you're saying that Liz *wanted* me to marry you? That's a crock. I don't believe that for one minute."

His glare was hateful.

"No," she said as she reached out to him. He recoiled.

"She just wanted a connection with you, the kids. And for some reason, she chose me to be it."

She touched his face, tried to make him look at her. "Listen, Bruce, she used me. I put my job in jeopardy just to bring her back information about you. Don't you understand? I felt so sorry for her, stuck in a child's body. God, I wish she hadn't confided in me. But she did. And for a year, I was the only person who knew her secret. I risked everything for her . . . and then, I fell in love," she said as she tried to make him look at her. ". . . with you."

At that, he drew back and let out a very audible sigh. "Why didn't she tell the doctor? And why you?"

"It's a long story."

"We have all night." He turned the light on at his side and stood up, shoulders back, square-jawed. "I want to know everything . . . the smallest detail."

She grabbed a tissue from the table, wiped her nose, and then nodded.

He shook his head slowly, but then said, "Let's go into the kitchen. I'll make some coffee. But I don't want the kids waking up, so we need to be quiet. I love you, but I don't know what to believe anymore."

She watched as he put on his slippers and robe. Then he motioned for her to follow.

Marcy didn't know how much longer she could stand the look of suspicion in Bruce's eyes as he sat across from her at the kitchen table. So far, he had questioned her every statement. As she sipped on her coffee, she tried to quell her emotions. She needed to convince him that her actions had been driven by passion, not subterfuge. Her marriage was at stake. Everything she held dear was in peril.

He must believe me. I never meant to fall in love with him. It just happened.

As Bruce listened to her explanations, Marcy tried to gauge his reactions, but couldn't discern whether he believed her or not.

Marcy bit her lip, and then asked the killer question. "I-if you could have her again, would you go back to her?" she asked. "I need to know where I stand."

She could just imagine what he saw as she sat before him with no makeup and swollen eyes. She was no longer the attractive, tall, willowy brunette he'd met eight years ago. She was middle-aged with small wrinkles lining her eyes and mouth, whereas Kate was young, beautiful, and talented.

Bruce looked at Marcy, as though comparing the two women. "I don't know what to think. Everything is upside down. Megan and Mark's mother is still alive . . . well, sort of." He stared past her, eyes squinted.

Marcy wondered if he still counted Adriana, Marcy's daughter, as theirs, or Shaun, the child they had borne together. Surely, they counted for something.

"Liz was my first love. You . . . you came in bearing gifts, as though you were her best friend. I was so easily taken in by your . . . your charade. *And* hers." He ran his fingers through his hair. "I'm so confused. I can't think clearly. I need time to work this out, time to figure out what's true and what's false."

She watched as he took a sip from his coffee mug, placed it carefully on the table and then cupped his chin in his hand. For a moment he looked as though he were staring a hole in the table.

"Well," she said as she rose from the table, "I've given you all the gruesome details. Now you have to decide whether our marriage is sacred to you, or if you want the young opera star, Ms. Kate Craig, for yourself."

She gave him a stern glance even as tears threatened to spill down her cheeks. "I saw how you looked at her. I'm pretty sure if you want her, you can have her. Just don't forget that we share a son and that during the last seven years we shared the raising of three other children together. *They* are not lies," she said, unable to hide the misery in her voice. "They are what we've weaved our lives around. Do I mean so little to you now that you are ready to abandon them?"

As she walked toward the kitchen door, she glanced back and noted that Bruce no longer looked so angry. Instead, his shoulders sagged and his eyes were downcast. The gray at his temples seemed coarser, and what had once been smile lines looked more like deep creases, as though he had aged overnight.

"I do love you, Bruce, believe it or not," she whispered. "And I never meant to deceive you or hurt you." She turned, reached out, and touched his shoulder but quickly took her hand away when she felt him recoil. "You have a decision to make. Don't take too long. I can't bear the . . ." Her throat constricted and she couldn't finish the sentence. She feared that if she ever did let go, the tears might never stop.

Chapter 13

Kate's Dilemma

Kate heard the automated garage door open and felt a chill run through her. She would finally get to be near her daughter, but at what cost? At the performance, she had seen the tension between Bruce and Marcy and knew that she had caused it. She flushed at the memory of Bruce's touch, then immediately felt guilty. Fate had dealt Kate a cruel hand, but now she was perpetuating it by getting in the middle of Bruce and Marcy's relationship. She looked at herself in the mirror that hung on the door to the garage, at her smooth, nineteen-year-old skin, her body at the height of its ability to attract men. What if *she* had been the one to age? What if Bruce had been attracted to a younger woman; how would she have felt in Marcy's position? She shuddered at the thought.

No, what she had done was wrong, but it wasn't wrong to want to see her daughter, to watch her grow into a woman. Surely Marcy would grant her that.

With a frisson of excitement, she stood next to the interior door that led to the garage and as it opened she stepped nearer. When Megan entered she reached out to touch the girl's arm in welcome. For the barbeque, Megan had dressed in jean cut-offs and a layered lacy cream-colored blouse, making her seem more mature than her seventeen years.

"Oh, Megan, I'm so glad you could make it," she said.

"Me too," Megan said as she looked at Josh, who was close on her heels.

Kate's heart skipped a beat as she ushered her one-time daughter through the elegant living room with an attached formal dining area and modern furniture done in soft pastels.

"There's no performance or rehearsal today, so I thought it would be a good chance to spend some time with my big brother. I've seen very little of you lately, since you've been at the University of Oregon and I've been back East." Kate realized that she was chattering on too fast, almost breathless, but she couldn't seem to slow down.

"Well, I'm here now, Sis," Josh said. Then, as though embarrassed by her blather, he quickly changed the subject. "So where are Mom and Dad?"

"They're outside. Mom's been in and out with food. She should be back in here any minute for another tray of goodies."

Kate noted that Megan was carrying something. "What's in the tin?"

"I made some cookies to bring to the barbeque," Megan said as she took the cookie tin into the kitchen and set it on the counter at Josh's direction. "They're cookies that my mom used to make for us," Megan said wistfully. "My favorites. They have a chocolate kiss inside them. I hope you'll like them."

Surprised by how deeply the word "mom" had affected her, Kate choked back a sob. Then she quickly fanned herself and tried to fake her sudden outburst into a coughing spasm. "Excuse me for a minute." She hurried to the bathroom, closed the door, and steadied herself with a hand on the counter. Warm tears dripped from her chin.

Mother's Surprise Cookies.

Liz's recipe, the same recipe Kate had given to Marcy to bake for Bruce and the kids shortly after she—no, *Liz* had died. The cookies were supposed to "prove" that Liz and Marcy had been "email" friends before the deadly accident, which would explain why he hadn't met her before her death. They had given Marcy entry into Bruce's life and trust. Now these prize cookies had come full circle.

Kate looked at herself in the mirror. She cursed her red and swollen eyes. Precious minutes were passing that she should be sharing with her daughter. She turned on the faucet, splashed cold water over her face, and patted her eyes with a tissue. She licked her lips and pinched her cheeks for color. As she did, she heard footsteps outside her door.

"Are you alright?" her mother asked. "I just came in to get something and heard you weren't feeling well."

"I'm fine. Something went down the wrong pipe. I'll be right out," Kate said in her brightest voice.

"Okay, but hurry. The party has started."

Kate paused until she heard her mother's footsteps fade then hurried down the hallway, through the kitchen, and out the back door.

By that time, Megan was already swimming in the pool with the other guests. Kate noted that she was graceful and powerful all at once . . . like she—Liz—had once been. Megan wore a one-piece suit that left no doubt that she was a well-developed woman. Kate's dad and brother were wearing swim trunks, matching T-shirts, sunglasses, and sandals. She listened to the male ritual as her dad and his friends, along with her brother, tried to light the barbeque. They were having the age-old debate about the right amount of chips to use for a full hickory flavor. As they threw more chips onto the already burning coals, the hickory aroma drifted through the air and added to the anticipation and hope that filled Kate. It was like an elixir.

Kate watched as her mom set the table and decorated it with early fall colors: red leaf maple, liquid amber, and even a yellowed sprig of aspen.

Eager to join the others, Kate pulled her shift over her head to reveal a two-piece swimsuit underneath. Then she kicked off her sandals and dove into the pool.

Her tall, muscular brother must have decided to leave the man-style cooking to Dad, because he soon took off his University of

Oregon Duck T-shirt and his flip-flops and joined them with a splash.

"You're a strong swimmer," Kate said to Megan.

"Thanks. I'm on the high school swim team. I guess I get it from my mother. She was Hayward High School's swim champ many years ago. I still have her trophies at home."

"I can tell you have it in your DNA. I love the water too. When I'm swimming I feel like a graceful bird flying through thick, silky air."

Funny how genetics worked with a different brain, Kate realized. She still liked and could do most of the things she'd done as Liz, and yet her taste in food was different from before. She absolutely loved seafood, whereas Liz had been allergic to shrimp and hated both the taste and smell of most seafood. The same was true with opera, only in reverse. She had loved it as Liz, but until she'd had Kate's voice, she'd had no way to display her passion other than to listen to it on her iPod.

She quelled her musings as she watched Josh dive beneath the surface and pop up between Kate and Megan, causing water to spout down on them like a fountain. "How lucky I am. My two favorite girls on either side of me," Josh said with a laugh. "You know, Megan, my sister is a great swimmer. Did you know that she once saved my life?"

"You did?" Megan said as she gawked at Kate. "What happened?"

Kate listened as Josh retold the story to Megan, but more than listening and nodding occasionally, she was watching the chemistry between Megan and her brother. Their eyes were riveted on each other. Kate had never seen her brother quite so animated. And she could see Megan hang on every word that Josh spoke as though it were of great consequence. He was obviously infatuated with Megan and she seemed equally smitten.

"Isn't that so?" Josh asked Kate.

Kate's mind had been on a different plane, but she could see that Josh was looking for confirmation. "Oh, yes," she said.

Later that night, when Kate stood out back, looking at the many stars twinkling in the night sky, she was filled with equal parts joy and dread. She loved Megan and Josh but she couldn't comprehend how the relationship between her brother and Megan could work. If they married, then her one-time daughter would be her sister-in-law and her brother would be her son-in-law. She rubbed her arms for warmth, shivering at the thought. At the same time, if they should marry, it would be the perfect fit for Kate to stay in touch with her family.

Chapter 14

Too Young

Bruce heard a car pull up. He walked to the front window, peered through a section of the blind, and watched as the too tall, too handsome Josh walked Megan to the door. Megan was giggling and her face was turned upward as she mooned at the young man. Josh seemed spellbound, his arm around Megan's waist and his eyes roving over her face.

Bruce wanted to open the door, shout "no" to them both and deck Josh. He knew he was being ridiculous, but it frightened him to think that his former wife—the cerebral part of her at least—might be a sister-in-law if the pair were to actually fall in love. Imagine family gatherings. Worse yet, the wedding. Which of the two women would give their daughter away? And how would he explain the situation to friends and family? But the thing that worried him most was that he would be in continued contact with his former wife, whom he had never stopped loving. Yes, he had tucked that part of himself away and moved on, but part of her had always been there, in his heart and in his memories each time he heard one of the kids say something that reminded him of her. Or when one of them would get a certain look that brought her to life again, if only for a moment. He closed his eyes, listening to the pair, then stepped back and waited. He had no idea what to say, how to tell them about the terrible path they were on. It was all too bizarre. He could barely believe the truth himself.

He heard a pause in their conversation—a long one. He pictured Josh kissing her. Then he heard, "Good night, Megan. I'll text you tomorrow."

Megan emitted a long sigh. Then, in a whispery voice Bruce heard her say, "I hope so. Good night, Josh." The word "Josh" seemed to hang in the air.

Bruce took another step backward as the door opened and then feigned surprise as Megan danced into the room, her face glowing.

"Well Megan, did you have a good time?" he asked, eyes cast downward to mask his spying.

"Oh, yes, Dad. It was . . . nice. They're such a tight family," she said as she closed the door. "Oh, and, Dad, Kate was there. She is *so* great."

"Really? How so?"

"Well, we talked, like, forever. It's so awesome," Megan said as she placed her purse and empty cookie tin on the coffee table and plopped onto the sofa. "You know, she's only two years older than me, but she's so-o-o mature."

"Oh?" Bruce said, wanting to press for more, but afraid to sound too eager.

Megan scooched down on the sofa and put her feet up on the coffee table. "And she's a hero. She actually saved her brother's life. It was a miracle because it happened only six months after that awful surgery. You know, doctors put a new brain in her."

"Yes, I heard about it." Bruce scratched his chin, his thoughts turning to the piece of paper he had signed, donating her organs to science. At the time, he had been so grief-stricken that he hadn't thought about the confidentiality agreement, the effect it might have on him not knowing where her organs had gone. He might have been naive, but he had assumed that they would use her organs in the normal way. He had never imagined they might use her brain in a transplant. Or that she might still have her memories.

"Anyway, like I said, she saved his life."

"Saved his life? How?"

"From what I understand he was fooling around, dove into a pool, and hit his head. Kate was in the shallow end. When he didn't come up, she swam to him and brought him to the surface. She even performed CPR."

"Really? She swam over and rescued him?" Bruce tried to hide his shock.

Megan nodded as she kicked off her flip-flops.

"What about Josh? Any plans to see him again?" he said, trying to play it cool.

"Could be. Where's Mom?" she said as she rose from the sofa, picked up the cookie tin, and walked toward the kitchen.

"Doin' laundry, I think," he said. But his mind was abuzz. His late wife, Liz, had been a champion swimmer, Hayward High School's number one swimmer and diver—a lifeguard. Ever since he had learned the truth he felt as though *he* were the one drowning. That *he* was the one in need of rescue.

Chapter 15

Who Do You Love?

Bruce wrapped his arms around his biceps. He ran his warm hands up and down his arms, but it didn't help. He still felt trapped. Was he Marcy's husband, or Liz/Kate's? This question gnawed at him constantly. He loved Marcy. She had been the best thing that could have happened to him after Liz's death. She was a great mother, a loving wife, and a true community advocate. She was a neighborhood watch leader president of the PTA, not to mention her achievements as a physical therapist.

But God help him, he still loved Liz. She was the mother of his children, his first love, and the most energetic and positive person he had ever known. She was passionate, ebullient, and charitable.

He loved them both. That was the bitter truth. So what now? *Should I approach Kate? Tell her what I know?*

He wrestled with this for several hours. Then he looked up Kate's itinerary and her performances on Google and friended her Facebook account. He sent a message:

Bruce Lindsay wants to meet with
Katherine Craig. Call or text me.
You know my cell phone number.

As he texted this information, he walked into Kaiser's cafeteria and poured himself a cup of its strong French roast coffee. He sat at a table by himself, sipped the hearty brew, and stared at his cell phone as though Kate were waiting for his message and would respond instantaneously.

He sat patiently, but nothing came. *Should I call her? Leave her a message?* He looked at his cell phone. Break time was almost over and he had to get back to the Imaging department where he was an X-ray tech.

He felt as though his life hung upside down. Nothing made sense anymore. His years with Marcy had been better than good. She was mature, sensible, and dependable. She was all of the things that Liz never was.

Liz was young, impressionable, giddy, and sometimes downright silly. Her hopes and dreams had bounced from one project to another. She would swing from high to low, depending upon the outcome of her ventures, and she always had a project: write a book, get a degree in something, sing a madrigal, sew a quilt, create a bronze sculpture of a dolphin.

Marcy was steady, sure, and serene. Liz was laughter, the great unknown and totally alive. Opposites, except for one thing: they were both sensual and an integral part of his life. When it came right down to it, he loved Marcy. There, he'd said it. He didn't want to lose her, but he needed to resolve the past first so that they could move on as a couple. So that all three of them could move on.

Later that night he heard a ding on his cellphone. He was in the kitchen while Marcy was in the living room. The message was from Kate. He stared.

Meet me at Val's Burgers in
Hayward at 11:30 tomorrow.
If you can't make it, text me.

He wrote back.

I'll be there

Chapter 16

Bruce and Kate

As Bruce entered the restaurant, he saw that Kate sat at a table to the right of the two windows under the big 7 Up sign. He hoped that no one in this best-in-the-west burger house would recognize an opera singer. The patrons were totally into burgers, baskets of sautéed mushrooms, hand-dipped ice cream, milkshakes, French fries, Cokes, football, and sandwiches. Even if some were into classical music, he doubted that anyone would know her.

Bruce felt at home in this place with its arched wooden beams and chrome ceiling fans. He'd known it since childhood.

He checked his wallet, remembering that the restaurant was a cash-only establishment—no credit cards. He smiled. *Some things never change.*

When Kate saw him, she smiled a somewhat nervous smile.

"Hi, Kate. How are you?" he asked as he slipped into one of the chairs opposite Kate. He noted that she had twisted a napkin, and then unrolled it, then had placed it carefully across her lap as though it were a very important part of her turquoise and white pantsuit.

"I'm okay, I guess," she responded.

Bruce was going through the motions, trying to figure out why he was there and what he hoped to accomplish that afternoon. It was grueling. Never in his life had he been so outraged by his own desires. He knew it was impossible for him to reconnect with Kate, or was it Liz? But he needed to know that she had accepted that verdict too. Was it closure that he was seeking? He was so confused.

Liz had once been her life. Was Kate back to connect with Mark and Megan, or was he still part of her dream?

He sat up straight and prayed to Almighty God for intervention. *Help me dear Lord to say the right things.*

He cupped his hands under his chin and leaned forward. "Hello, Kate," he said. "Or should I say Liz? It is you, isn't it?"

Kate's lips were trembling. She simply nodded.

"I think I figured that out many years ago when you sang at the college. But I couldn't deal with the truth back then." He looked directly into her eyes.

He reached out and touched her hand.

Kate shuddered but finally found her voice. "You have no idea what I've been through. At first it was pure agony, not seeing you or the kids." She clutched the napkin with her free hand. "I did everything I could to find a way to see you, to see Megan and Mark . . . just to know that my family was okay. It was horrible. There were times that I wished I didn't have the memories. And then there were days, hundreds of days that soon turned into years, when I knew that those memories were what kept me alive. I prayed for understanding. I prayed that I would wake up and learn that it was all a bad dream."

"Kate, look at yourself. You're a young, successful woman, traveling the world. I'm a middle-aged man with teenagers, a young son, a mortgage, and a wife."

She cleared her throat, blinked. "How well I know." She withdrew her hand and smoothed out her napkin again.

"You two ready to order?" asked the young waiter.

Bruce looked up, but Kate looked straight ahead and answered, "Two coffees, one with cream and sweetener and one black."

Bruce interjected. "Hold the cream and sweetener, just two black." He leaned forward. "You see, Kate, some things change."

The waiter turned his head to one side. "Yes, sir, coming right up. But if you and your *daughter* want to try something really great, we have the best burgers in town."

"Yes, we know," they both said at the same time.

The waiter shrugged, winked at Kate, and walked away to fill their order.

Bruce chuckled. "You see, folks think I'm having coffee with my daughter. Nothing is the same. Life isn't reversible." He sighed deeply, almost a moan. "Kate, listen, as Liz you were my world. You were . . . it. But then one day, suddenly, you were gone. All I had left were memories."

"Memories. Ah, yes, just like the Broadway show *Cats* . . . and a new life shall begin," she sang softly.

"Eight years ago I would have given anything to have you back. But that was eight long years ago. Today I'm married to Marcy, thanks to you. And she's a good wife."

Kate lifted her chin and ran her tongue over her dry lips. "Do you love her the way you loved me?" she asked.

The waiter put the coffees on the table. "Will there be anything else?"

"That's all," Bruce said.

He turned his attention back to Kate and shook his head. "No two loves are ever the same, because no two people are the same." He looked down at his wedding ring. "I've wrestled over the question of what to do about Marcy—about you. What if I had the choice? Marcy and I have had our disagreements and conversations about you. It isn't easy, but I love her and she's the woman I want to spend the rest of my life with." He looked up at the ceiling. "There. I've said it. So now what?"

Kate let out what sounded like a sigh of relief. "I understand," she said. "But in order to move forward, I think we need a plan."

"Oh?" he said, tilting his head slightly.

"Yes." She held up a hand and extended her index finger. "First, our children must never know, agreed?"

He gave her a nod.

"I love them so much, but this would be too hard for them to bear. At the same time, I hope you and Marcy will please keep me informed, find a way that I can see Mark and Megan from time to time and, if they ever need anything, and you think I can help, please let me know . . . especially Mark. He's almost a man now and I haven't seen him except in pictures on Marcy's Facebook."

Again, Bruce nodded and said, "Done."

She joined her index finger with her middle finger. "Second, I don't know what to do about Josh and Megan. I do enjoy her friendship. And they do seem good for each other. I know you and Marcy feel differently, but for now, I hope you will sit back and see where it goes. Who knows, they could be on to their third relationship by this time next year. The more we push, one way or the other, the more they will gravitate to each other, don't you think? So let's just give them a little space for now."

"I'll talk to Marcy—see what we can do," he said before she could launch into her next point.

She seemed to pause for effect and then she added her ring finger to the first two. "Third, I want you to know that Marcy is the best friend I ever had. I'm glad you have a good woman. Cherish her."

She raised her little finger. "Forth, I'm paying the bill, so I suggest you indulge in one of those monster burgers and some onion rings." She released a nervous laugh.

Bruce smiled and countered back, "First, I agree we must keep it a secret. Second, I know better than to forbid Josh and Megan from dating. She's too much like you. That wouldn't work at all." He curled a lip, Elvis style, and added, "As far as Mark goes, perhaps we can invite you to a picnic or some other family function so that you can see how well our son is doing, though it may be a while until Marcy feels more comfortable with everything. Third, I know what Marcy did for you and I can assure you, I know how lucky I am. Fourth, I'll take you up on the burger and the onion rings, but only if you'll eat half."

Kate tented her eyebrows. "I agree."

Bruce motioned to the waiter and ordered the biggest burger on the menu, onion rings and coffee refills. Then he turned to Kate. "What about that Giovanni character? You care about him?"

Kate turned her head and thought for a moment. "He's handsome and has a great voice, but no . . . he's not my type," she said wistfully, as she lowered her head and peered into her coffee cup, which was still half full.

Bruce reached across the table, lifted her chin until she was at eye level with him. "Be careful, Kate. He's way too smooth. In my opinion, he has all the earmarks of a libertine. Tread carefully."

"You don't understand. It's lonely when you're on the road all the time. I don't love Giovanni, but we do have a common love of the opera. It's a strong link." Then she looked into Bruce's eyes and added, "Could it be you're just a little bit jealous?"

"No. It's just fatherly advice."

CHAPTER 17

A LONELY HEART

Kate went back to the solitary confinement of her hotel room and studied her upcoming travel plans. As she reviewed the itinerary, she thought about her meeting with Bruce. In her heart of hearts, she knew that they had done the right thing, that there was no going back, only forward.

But then she recalled the phrase in their wedding vows, "Until death do we part." She had died . . . but had she really?

Marcy didn't know just how lucky she was. Bruce was a perfect catch, a beautiful soul. Kate missed him. She often dreamed about him. But when she would wake up, she would chastise herself. Her life was here, fulfilling the dream she'd had as Liz all those years ago. She just hadn't realized the repercussions of that dream—the abject loneliness of life on the road.

God help me. He isn't mine any more.

She wondered about Gino. They had gone out on a few dates. Was he just a stand-in for now? She knew he was an incorrigible flirt, but the opera scene hadn't offered many opportunities to meet other eligible bachelors. And since the past several months they had been paired for performances in Europe and the States, he had been the one constant person in her life. If it hadn't been for his companionship, she would have felt even lonelier. He had been more attentive recently, less flirtatious with other women.

Does he really care about me, or is it just an act?

Kate felt secluded. Her performances would take her around the world and back, but time spent with friends and family was so intermittent that it barely counted. Texts, Facebook accounts, emails, and phone calls helped, but all of them lacked the personal warmth of a hug.

Gino was the only man she could date since most of the other performers were either married or too old.

Why had she chosen this career path? It was a solitary life, a lonely life. But she always fell back on the truth: it was the music itself that sustained her. It was her soul food. If only she could find someone to share it with. Someone to love.

Kate called room service. "Would you please send me up a bowl of soup?" . . . "Yes, it's okay." . . . "Yes, I know it's two a.m. Thanks."

Chapter 18

Thank Heavens

Marcy was waiting in the living room when she heard the garage door open. She knew where Bruce had been for the last several hours. She wasn't sure how to act.

How do you broach the subject when your husband has met with a young, beautiful woman who had once been his wife?

For the moment, her only consolation was that at least he hadn't lied to her when she had asked him where he was going.

That afternoon, knowing that he would be meeting with Kate, Marcy had been especially careful with her hair and makeup. She wanted to look as attractive as possible without going overboard. She certainly didn't want to look stressed.

So, when he entered the room, Marcy tried to look as though she had been engrossed in reading the newspaper. She lowered the paper, looked up and asked, "How'd it go?"

He walked toward her. "It was good. Where are the kids?"

"Shaun is next door playing with Eric. The girls and Mark went to the movies. It's just us."

Bruce sat next to her, removed the newspaper from her hands, and placed it on the table. He took her hand, raised it to his lips, and kissed it gently.

"Everything is fine. Everything is perfect. And you are the one and only woman in my life."

Marcy felt a sob rise from her throat. It was as though all the tension from the past several months had just shot into Neverland. Bruce put his arms around her and she felt herself melt into him. She listened as he recounted his meeting with Kate and her requests.

"I'm on board, so now what?" Marcy asked, feeling as though a huge weight had been lifted from her shoulders.

"I have an idea, Mrs. Lindsay." Bruce emphasized the word *Mrs.* "Although I had a hearty lunch, I think we should get a sitter for tonight, and I should take my best girl out for dinner and dancing. So what do you think about that? We can plan devious ways to break up Megan's and Josh's relationship. We can make a list—check it twice."

"Naughty and nice," she replied.

Part II

Memories

Chapter 19

Secrets

Noah flicked off the computer screen, his mind churning in a thousand directions. *World Class Neurosurgeon Performs First Successful Brain Transplant Surgery.* Once he had read that, he had scrolled through and read every article he could find on the man he had been playing chess with daily for several weeks now. He had never talked so openly and candidly with anyone in his life before this. For the first time since he'd come down with his disease, he'd felt hopeful.

He heard the door open and his mother's voice as she greeted the man he was just reading about online.

"Noah, Dr. Jamison is here 'ta see ya," his mother called.

"I'll be in, in a jif," Noah called, wheeling his wheelchair toward the door that had been widened to accommodate his special needs. Soon, the accommodations would no longer be needed. Time was running out. Day by day he had watched himself shrivel into a shell of his former self. His skin had grown more ashen; his voice had become hoarse. Even the effort to push himself around in his chair had him wheezing and out of breath. One day, in the not-too-distant future, the illness would catch up with him, unless . . .

By the time he met Jamison, who was already seated beside the chess table and sipping on the aromatic orange spiced tea that Noah's mother had served, he could barely speak he was so winded.

"May . . . take me a . . . sec . . . to catch me . . . breath," he said, feeling suddenly lightheaded.

The last thing he remembered was a sinking darkness and pitching forward in his wheelchair. He awoke to find his mother wailing and Dr. Jamison trying to calm her as he checked Noah's vital signs as best he could with the limited equipment available.

"How are you feeling?" Dr. Jamison asked, worry lines marring his forehead.

"Not . . . too . . . good," Noah admitted. "Ya might have a chance at winnin' this time," he added, trying to make light of what he knew was a serious situation.

"Ya gave us a right good scare, son," his mother said, still hovering over the doctor's shoulder. "Can't ya do somethin' for him, Doc? He's our only son, he is. I can't bear the thought 'a losing him."

Dr. Jamison frowned. "I wish I could. Believe me, if I could I would . . . ."

"But . . . ya could . . . if ya wanted to," Noah pleaded, holding out hope that the doctor could see that he had so much to offer the world—that he would repay the doctor ten-fold in the life that he led. "I read . . . ." he said, his words interrupted by a fit of coughing. He tried again. "I read . . . that you can perform . . . transplants. Brain transplants."

He closed his eyes, feeling dizzy again. When he opened them, he could see tears welling up in the doctor's eyes.

"The deaths musta been hard on ya, no?"

The doctor stilled, then finally nodded, his lips pursed.

"But see, the thing is . . . ." Noah paused to catch his breath. "I will die without a transplant. And I . . . have so much to give . . . to the . . . world. Maybe . . . even . . . a cure . . ." He groaned, frustrated at the effort to speak. ". . . for this disease."

Dr. Jamison turned away, but Noah could see that he had touched the man's heart.

Noah's mother put a hand on the doctor's shoulder, and with a kindness that had given Noah peace throughout his ordeal, she spoke softly to the doctor, each word no doubt carefully chosen, if he knew anything at all about his mum.

"I know we can't expect ya to play God, Dr. Jamison. And we'll understand if ya cannot do anythin'. But . . ." She paused as if to gather her courage. "Our boy is a good boy. He has a gifted mind. A mind given him by God hisself. So ya can understand, can't you, that it's hard for us . . . to accept what has happened."

The doctor nodded, looking much older than he had when Noah had first seen him seated at the table.

Though weak still, Noah reached out and put a hand on the doctor's arm. "It's all right, Doc. Whatever you decide. You will . . . always . . . be a . . . good friend. You have made . . . these last few . . . weeks . . . bearable." A tear fell down his cheek unbidden. "Thanks for . . . being there for . . . me."

"But it makes so much more sense to me now," Jamison said as he paced back and forth leaving footprints on Inna's normally immaculate carpet. He'd been taking tea with Noah for several weeks now, but seeing him as he had today, lying on the floor, cyanosis turning his lips blue, he'd been shocked into remembering that the boy didn't have long to live. Not unless he did something to help him. The thought of him wanting to become a doctor, like Jamison, fueled something in him that hadn't been there before. This boy was a genius. He could save lives, if given the chance. If Jamison had ever had a son, he would have wanted a boy just like Noah—curious, brilliant, but most of all kind.

"There are young men with healthy bodies that are brain-dead. And here's Noah with a marvelous brain but a withering body. Why not try another transplant? The families of both would finally have some hope . . . a healthy life they can each share."

Inna cocked her head in disbelief. "But darling, it will start up all over again. Sure, Kate's surgery was successful. But remember how they vilified you when the subsequent surgeries failed? Remember the protesters?" She pulled up the sleeves of her pale yellow sweater that contrasted with the black skirt and stockings she wore. "And you haven't performed surgery in years. Your license is no longer valid."

Jamison stopped his pacing and took a seat on the familiar brown leather couch with its plaid knit throws and plush pillows.

"But I won't do the surgery. Doctor Johnson is head of neurology at Stanford now. She assisted in the surgery with Kate and the others. And once she knows the secret behind Kate's success—the fact that her memory wasn't erased and that's what kept her alive rather than simple luck—*she* can do it."

He leaned forward as Inna placed a cup of tea on a trivet before him.

"You think so?"

"I do."

Inna poured a cup of pekoe for herself, then sat down in the accent chair opposite him. "I know that you've become attached to Noah over the past few weeks, and you're doing this for him, but what about Kate? As far as I know, we're the only two people besides Kate and her therapist that know about her donor memories. When this gets out, what will happen to her?" she asked with a frown. "And what will happen to us?"

"Does that matter? What about Noah? He could have a long and fruitful life. I want him to live. I want him to realize his dreams." Jamison rose and walked over to his wife and embraced her. "I couldn't bear to lose him knowing I could prevent his death. Besides, it's not the same. We know what caused the other deaths now, so we can prevent it. And he will die anyway without the transplant."

Inna wrapped her arms around him and kissed him on the cheek, obviously conflicted with the choice. "Think through this carefully, Donald, because what you do from this point on will have repercussions. Maybe even unforeseen ones. Make sure you're doing it for the right reason . . . for him and not for yourself," she said with a tone of resignation then gently pushed him away and looked deep into his eyes.

"You're right, I know," he said, taking her hand. "But I can't let this go, Inna. I couldn't live with myself knowing I could help this boy. You've got to understand," he pleaded. "I'll do what I have to do to keep him alive. But I promise you this—I *will* have a talk with Kate. She needs to know. The media will be all over her . . . wanting to know everything, who she was, what she did. And with her level of celebrity, it could be daunting."

"It could be worse than daunting," Inna countered. "Just be careful, Donald. Promise me."

"I will," he said, giving his wife another short embrace. Then he walked into the kitchen, took a pad and pencil from a drawer and sat down at the oak table. He ran his hand over the distressed wood and felt a kinship. *Priority list. I need a priority list.*

In a scrawl that only a doctor can achieve he wrote a list:

- *Talk with Kate. Tell her about the life she can save.*
- *Call Doctor Johnson. Tell her the truth about Kate.*
- *If Johnson will concede, tell Noah*
- *Move quickly. Noah doesn't have much time*
- *Try to protect Kate and us from the press*

Chapter 20

Doctor Makes a House Call

Jamison didn't even shave. He felt the gray stubble on his chin and shook his head. So what? He had more important things to do than to shave. This would be a hallmark day.

He sat at his computer and googled "Katherine Craig Soprano." He wasn't wild about computers, but he found that they offered easy access to information and connections, something he needed. Several sites appeared on the screen: upcoming performances, Wikipedia references, reviews, and more. But he was looking for one that would provide contact information.

After several attempts, he found a site for fans and invited Kate to friend him—he wasn't even sure what that meant but thought it couldn't hurt—then clicked on "Contact." He thought about what he should write, how to let her know to contact him.

He filled in the required information and typed in the letters that spelled nothing to prove that he was a real person, then wrote,

URGENT. Please respond as soon as possible. Need your help. Text me. Must talk with you ASAP. Donald Jamison MD—your neurosurgeon.

He added the last line in case an agent or someone other than Kate herself scanned messages before forwarding them on to her. He added his email address, his home address, and his phone number.

"Any luck?" Inna asked as she entered his study.

"I don't know. But if she doesn't respond within the next three days, I think we should make arrangements to fly back to the states. I must have this conversation with her. Noah doesn't have much time. Any delays could quash all chances."

Inna grimaced. "So, everything will be left up to Kate? The chance for Noah and others to have a full life, you'll leave it all up to her?"

Jamison pushed the keyboard aside and shook his head. "No. But I'll feel much better if she becomes party to it. When the world learns that memory is essential to a successful brain transplant . . . I guess I should say *body* transplant, it could damage her and others. I need to consider her, consider her feelings and that of both families. The Craigs could feel cheated. After all, they didn't choose for Kate to keep her memories as Liz. It would be like losing Kate all over again, once they learn the truth. And as far as I know, Bruce Lindsay doesn't even know about the transplant. What a mess."

Inna nodded as she put on a belt that accentuated her slim waistline. "You've become a wonderful softy in your old age," she chided lovingly as she walked over to him and placed a manicured hand on his shoulder. "But what about Noah? Are you going to say anything to him about what you're up to?"

At that moment, Rosie, the Jamisons' dog, put both her front paws on his knee and stared up at him. She licked her lips, a behavior that said, "Feed me. I need a treat." Jamison absentmindedly scratched the fluffy Lhasa-poodle behind the ear. Then to Inna he said, "No. Not until and unless I have something substantial to offer. But I will call Doctor Johnson. She needs to know the truth. The operation was successful many years ago, and it will be again. Under the right circumstances, she can lead the way."

"Wrong. *You* led the way. She can just take it to the next level. Someday the operation may be as accepted as the heart transplant is today." She pointed at the dog still pleading for a meal. "By the way, your 'hound' wants your attention, Darling. Better find her a treat soon."

Jamison looked down at the little rescue-mongrel, sighed, and smiled. Rosie was a mature dog when they'd adopted her—probably seven or eight years old. She was partially deaf, riddled with non-cancerous growths, and she was the second love of his life. She was his constant companion when Inna was out doing her thing.

Rosie followed him everywhere, laid at his feet when he sat, and slept at the foot of his bed at night. She offered unconditional love, something he needed. So, yeah, in return he'd fed her and spoiled her.

He thought about how he'd become such a sentimental person. Now, as the years had mellowed him, he'd found that all life had more meaning. Instead of killing spiders, he would take them outside and bid them farewell. If ants invaded, he'd find what they were after and move the morsels outside, coaxing them to leave. He just didn't want to kill anything—with the exception of mosquitoes and flies. They were still fair game. And yet he'd had to deal with probably *the* most difficult ethical dilemma of his life—to ask family members to donate the body of a deceased loved one for the chance at life for someone sure to die. The only way he'd been able to resolve the dilemma in his mind was to realize that one was already dead, and the other would surely die without the surgery. At least this way, one of them had a chance at life, and for that he was willing to risk moral outrage, if necessary.

"Okay, Rosie, you win," he said as he got up from his desk. "Come on, girl. Let's go see what's in the pantry."

Rosie wagged her tail, ran her tongue over the outside of her mouth in anticipation of something delicious, and trailed her master.

Inna followed them into the kitchen and poured herself a cup of coffee. "So when will you contact Dr. Johnson?" she asked.

He recalled the last time he'd seen Dr. Johnson. She'd been a stately looking African-American woman with a shaved, nicely shaped head. She had a slight limp that she had told him was the result of a skiing accident she'd been in when she was sixteen. He figured she'd be in her early fifties now, and her two sons would be teenagers.

Jamison pulled a box of dog biscuits from the pantry and joined Inna at the kitchen table. He broke one of the treats in half and gave it to Rosie. "I'll contact her soon. But first I need to know what I'm going to say—how I'm going to tell this story and how I'm going to convince her to help Noah. My guess is that her first response will be 'I need proof.' That's what I would have said."

"So what's the proof?" Inna asked.

"It's Kate."

"So will you wait until she responds?"

"I'll wait. But three days is my limit. Every day Noah grows weaker. So I won't wait long," he said as he reached down and gave Rosie the other half of the biscuit.

Chapter 21

Kate's Dilemma

Kate's cell phone rang next to the bedside in her hotel room. For a moment, she forgot which city she was in, but then remembered. New York, the Big Apple. She rolled over, looked at the screen, saw the name Cassie Bailey appear, and picked it up.

"Hi, Cass. What's up?"

"There was a strange message on your Internet fan site," Kate's manager said. "A Doctor Jamison, the surgeon who did the transplant, wants to talk with you. He wants to call you, says it's urgent. But he's in Australia and needs to know when he can speak to you . . . you know, Pacific Standard Time and all that."

Stunned, Kate's eyes went wide and her mouth went dry. "What in the world? What could he want with me after all these years?" She hadn't seen or heard from him since he had set her up with her current doctor. It had been rumored that he had moved to Australia, but she had never learned if that were true until now.

"I dunno what he wants. But I'll forward the message to you. It has his email address and phone number."

How could anything be so urgent after seven long years? Kate heard a ding announcing a new email message and opened it up. *A message from Dr. Jamison.* She stared at the words for several minutes, trying to decide whether to call him or delete it. After a numb moment, she decided to text him a short query.

Subject: Hello?

Text: My manager received a fan-page message from you. You want me to call you? Why?

She hadn't expected a response so soon. She had assumed that it was the middle of the night in Australia. But within seconds she read,

Must talk with you. It's a life or death matter. No one else. Just you and me. Call me any time. I'll explain.

Life or death matter? Kate couldn't imagine what he was thinking. Had he gone mad? And why "no one else"? What was the big secret?

Kate got up and paced the room. She was keenly aware that he knew the memory erasure hadn't worked. *He can ruin everything for me if I'm not careful.* She had stolen a second chance at life, now that she was finally getting to see her daughter again. His timing couldn't have been worse, and yet she felt certain that he wouldn't have contacted her with such an urgent request if the stakes weren't high.

She picked up her smartphone and looked at it for several seconds, laid it back down, and then picked it up again. After a moment's hesitation, she pressed the button to engage the phone and carefully punched in the country code and number. It rang.

Their conversation lasted less than ten minutes, but Kate felt as though she had aged twenty years by the time it ended.

"I have a boy in urgent need," he said after the summary introductions. "He needs surgery now, if he is to survive. You have to understand, if you don't take the lead on this within three days, I am going to go to the press and get this done."

She paced the floor, counted the tiles in the entranceway, her thoughts spinning. *Is he blackmailing me? What to do?* There was no way out.

He still has the note I wrote seven years ago—so that he would understand why the subsequent surgeries had failed, why the others had died; the one I wrote so he would stop the transplants. It said,

I am alive because you made a
mistake. I have the memory of the
donor. I know who I once was.
The others died because the brain
erasers were successful.
Stop the brain transplants now!

It was supposed to remain a secret. Only Marcy knew before that. She was the first to understand what had happened, the one who had figured out that the donor memory was what made the transplant work. Kate had always tried to understand the concept of hell. Now she understood.

What will my Craig family think? They had believed that they would be getting their daughter back once the circuitry of her brain had reconfigured to the Kate persona. That she would be the person she had been before the disease had withered her brain.

Will they still love me if they know I have Liz's brain in Kate's body?

And what of her two kids? What would they think once they knew the truth? Would they embrace her, want her back, or would they shun her as an aberration of nature, a Frankenstein of a person who was neither Liz *nor* Kate. And yet both, in some respects.

She covered her face. She was a lie. Her whole existence as Kate was a lie.

At that moment, she hated Jamison. "He has no right, God!" she shouted as tears flooded over her cheeks. She sobbed so long, so hard, that her ribcage ached and the hotel's satin pillow that she had clutched to her chest was tear-stained.

Three days. Either way I choose, I lose.

Chapter 22

Believe It or Not

Kate deliberately put one foot in front of the other hoping to build her confidence as she approached the Information Counter at Stanford Hospital in search of Dr. Johnson, the African-American woman who had worked alongside Dr. Jamison all those years ago. Of the three neurosurgeons that participated in the surgery, she had been the only one who had treated her as a human being, not just a case.

"I have an appointment to see Dr. Johnson in neurosurgery," she said.

The volunteer, a sweet grandmotherly woman with graying hair and tiny lips coated in light coral lipstick, grinned up at Kate.

"You're Katherine Craig, aren't you?" she asked. "We've been waiting for you. I mean the doctor has been waiting to see you." Her eyes crinkled as she touched Kate's hand. "Actually everyone's been waiting to catch a glimpse of you. You're a celebrity and a walking miracle."

Kate glanced at the volunteer's badge and said, "Thank you, Mrs. White. Where should I go?"

The volunteer gave her directions to a conference room. Kate followed the woman's instructions to a room at the end of a long hallway. When she opened the door, she saw a bank of doctors seated at a table. In each of her earlier follow-up sessions, it had been just her doctor and her in the exam room, nothing like this.

"Oh, I'm sorry. I must be in the wrong place. I . . ." Then she saw Dr. Johnson at the head of the room and panicked, turning abruptly.

"No, Miss Craig. Please come in. I hope you don't mind. I wanted certain members of the medical staff to meet you."

Kate stood with her mouth agape. No way was she about to bare her soul to this room full of strangers. Sure, the word would eventually get out. The media would pounce on this scandal. She needed more time, more support, and she wanted to pick her own terms in releasing the information.

Then she realized that running from this room could start a buzz sooner than she wanted. So she turned around. "Sorry. I thought I was in the wrong place."

"Come in, Miss Craig. Do you mind if I call you Kate?" Dr. Johnson asked.

"N-no, that's fine," she said as she inched back into the room. She counted heads. Thirteen. Not a lucky number.

After twenty minutes of friendly questions about headaches and other "problems" she might be having and accounts of her singing—celebrity questions she had answered so many times over the years that she could barely stand one more—they followed up with more difficult questions about her emotional well-being that left her sweaty and fatigued. Always before, she had acted the part of a child, told them what she thought they wanted her to hear. Today she tried to be more candid without giving away too much.

After another twenty minutes of grueling questions, she announced, "I do need to get back soon to prepare for tonight's performance. But I was wondering if I could have a word with you, Dr. Johnson, in private before I leave?"

One by one, the other physicians came over, shook her hand, and left the room. She faced Dr. Johnson alone.

"Come sit over here by me Kate, and tell me why you really came."

Kate swallowed and prayed for heavenly intervention. None came. "I've come to tell you why I survived and the other patients didn't."

Dr. Johnson sat back in her chair and raised her hand to her mouth as though to stifle a gasp. "You think you know why you lived and the other brain-transplant patients didn't?"

"I think so."

Kate felt some small relief as she unburdened herself from the lies. She told her everything, and then asked for her silence on the matter. She needed a chance to tell her family before the media pounced, providing 24/7 coverage and prying into her past life. That would be especially true if and when the transplant surgeries resumed.

"Kate, you don't need to tell me any more," Dr. Johnson said. "For some time, I've thought that memory was important. A colleague and I did some experimental transplants on animals. We used brain-dead animals and others with extreme physical disabilities. We never thought to erase their memories, but the rest of the procedure was the same as the one we did on you. And most survived. So I thought memory erasure might be the problem. Now you've confirmed it."

"One more thing," Kate said. "Dr. Jamison wants you to call him. He says it's a matter of life and death."

"Oh?" Dr. Johnson replied, frowning.

Kate handed her a slip of paper, thanked her for her cooperation, and then left the room feeling as though her world was about to crash down around her.

Chapter 23

The Truth Will Come Out

During the drive from Stanford, Kate hardly noticed the Halloween decorations around the storefronts. Fall and the coming holidays had always been her favorite time of the year. But instead of singing, she practiced what she would say. Her family needed to know the truth before word got out, before they were all blindsided by the media. They needed to hear it from her . . . in her words. But would they, could they, understand?

Kate glanced at the golden leaf wreath on the door and wiped her shoes on the welcome mat. She opened the door to her parents' home and called out, "Mom, Dad, I'm home. I need to talk to you."

"We didn't expect you today," Donna Craig said as she entered the living room from the kitchen. She wiped her hands on her apron that was dusted with flour and smeared here and there with what looked like butter. "I've been making cookies for the church bake sale." Then her mother seemed to catch the drift that something was amiss because she looked at her with concern. "Honey, you look pale. What's wrong?"

"There's something I need to tell you and Dad . . . and Josh. It's important," she said, her voice breaking. She knew that they loved her, but would they still love her once she told them the truth?

"I'll go get your dad," her mother said. "He's in the garage tinkering with something. Sit down. You look like you're about to fall over."

Kate collapsed onto the couch and pulled the crocheted throw onto her lap, wishing she could hide the truth, withhold the pain that was sure to follow.

Her father trailed her mother into the room, his face tanned and the lines on his forehead revealing his worry. "Your mother says you have something important to tell us. Are you okay?"

"S-sort of," she stammered. "This isn't easy. I was hoping I could keep this from you, but I can't. Not anymore."

Her mother came over to the couch and sat down beside her. She put her hand on Kate's flushed face. "Kate, you're scaring us. Tell us, what is it? Are you sick?"

Kate looked down at the throw she was holding, unable to look them in the eyes. The tears that she had been holding back now ran slowly, but steadily, down her cheeks. "I've been living a lie for these past eight years. I'm so afraid you won't love me anymore when you learn what I have to tell you." She choked back tears.

Her father took a seat opposite them and leaned forward, the worry evident on his forehead. "Nothing you could say would ever cause us to stop loving you. You're our daughter. We stand with you, no matter what."

Kate tried to hide the doubt in her eyes. "Eight years ago, when I awoke in the recovery room, I didn't know who either of you were. A mistake was made during the preparation for surgery. The personal memory of the donor brain that I received was supposed to be erased. But something went wrong. When I awoke, I had the memories of a former life."

Her mother and father sat forward and stared at her, Donna's eyes growing wide. "Oh good Lord," she said. "Why . . . why didn't you tell someone? Why now after all these years?"

"I was afraid the surgeons would try to correct their mistake. And I thought if they did that, then I would truly be dead. Here's the truth: apparently those memories are what helped me survive the surgery. As you know, all the other transplant patients died.

My memory is what made me fight harder . . . I wanted so badly to live."

Her father's face crumpled in disbelief. He shook his head and ran a weathered hand across his forehead. "What did you remember? Who were . . . *are* you?"

"I can only recall some things." She had rehearsed this line because she wasn't ready to tell them the whole truth. She wanted to protect Bruce and her kids as long as possible. "At first the memories were strong. I know that I was a college student and that my mother died a few years before the transplant. I no longer remember what she looks like. Now when I hear the word 'mother' I see only your face," she said as she looked lovingly at Donna. At least that part was true.

Donna stood up, then knelt beside Kate and wrapped her arms around her. She looked over at her husband and searched his face, then turned her head to Kate. "Darling child . . ." She fought back tears. "It's hard to hear those words, I must admit. We loved our daughter more than words can say. And I won't deny it may take me a little time to wrap our heads around this, but I'm not sorry that you came into our lives," she said as she added her own tears to Kate's. "You have been a blessing, each and every day. I can't say I will get over this right away. But it's easier to accept the loss knowing that you are still our daughter. You *are* still ours, aren't you?"

Kate nodded through tears.

At that point, John Craig, who had been silent until now, came and knelt beside them both. The trio wrapped their arms around each other. Kate clutched them both to her and felt a weight drop from her burdened shoulders, her sins cleansed.

After several minutes of reassurance from her parents, her father asked, "Why, after all these years, tell us this now?"

Kate told them about Jamison's call and what he had forced her to do. She recapped her meeting with Dr. Johnson and told them about Jamison's overall plan.

Kate held her parents' hands in hers. "Mom, Dad, if they resume the transplants, you can imagine how the media will be. They'll be all over us again. And this time they will know that memories must be intact in order for the patient to survive. The media will hound me for information about my past life. It could be really tough."

"You, dear daughter, don't need to say anything to them. We will stand by your side. *'No Comment'* is all that we will say. It's all *you* need to say. No—I take that back—you can add Happy Thanksgiving, Merry Christmas, and have a Happy New Year."

"And Josh?" Kate asked. "When and how do I tell him?"

"You won't have to do that alone," John said. "I'll call him and ask him to come over, and we'll do that together, as a family."

At that moment, Kate looked at the praying angel that graced the fireplace mantel and felt a powerful surge of love.

Chapter 24

Young Love

The ding on her smart phone alerted Megan to a text message from Josh:

Sorry cant C U 2day, something
w/fam came up. Catch u later.

Her heart dropped. Despite her parents' strong objections, everything had been going so great. Maybe their attitude was what made her dig in and pursue Josh with such determination.

As she sat at the edge of her bed, she scrolled through the dozens of selfies they had taken. She felt sure that they were "a thing." Weird, though, that he hadn't said more. She wrote back:

What a grind. Wanna C U soon.

She fell back on her bed, feet dangling over the side and recalled their recent days together. Their relationship was speeding up. It was time to start slowing things down a bit. She remembered how young her mother had been when she and Mark were born and how her mom had been trying to go back and get her education. She didn't want to go down the same route. Fortunately, Josh was going to school to be an EMT, and Megan . . . well, she would decide what she wanted to be once she went to college.

Maybe I should break it off. Maybe I should enter a convent. HA!

She sighed, shifted off the bed and walked barefoot to Adriana's room. Knocked. "Can I come in?"

"Enter at your own risk," Adriana replied.

"I need someone to talk to, but not Mom or Dad. They're always on my case," Megan said.

"So what's up, little sister?" Adriana asked as she rushed to put down her iPad and then hit the off button, almost as though she had something to hide.

Megan sat on the edge of Adriana's bed, picked up the empty cup on the side table and ran her finger around its smooth lip. "Josh was going to pick me up today. We were going to hang out for the day and maybe go out for a bite, maybe a movie. But he texted me. Said something came up with his family. I don't mean to be an emo, but I feel like something bad is gonna happen—just a, whadaya call it? 'Premonition' I guess."

"Listen, you're too tight with him anyway," she said, flashing Megan a pointed look. "You're going to lose it if you don't back up. Know what I mean? Give him some space, Meg."

"I know I should. But I think I love him." With that, she plunked down the cup and sprawled back on the bed.

"You are so hormonal. It's not love and it won't last. He'll be back to college. And you need to finish high school, ya know? Think about it. Look at me," she said, pointing two fingers at her eyes. "Am I right?"

Megan clamped both hands over her face and moaned. "I could just die. Life's not fair. And I do, I do love him soooo much."

"Well, if it's true love with a capital L, it'll still be there when you've graduated college and gotten your degree."

Adriana was such a big sister. For once, couldn't she just see Megan's point of view? Still, she was okay . . . for an older sister, by all of four months.

"Whatever," Megan said, and she grabbed the pillow from the bed and tossed it playfully at Adriana. "Thanks anyway," she said.

Then she got up and trudged out of her sister's room, no wiser than she was before she'd entered.

It was 10:00 p.m. when Megan's smart phone rang. She looked at the screen: Josh Craig. *Strange, he never calls, just texts.* She swiped to answer, "Josh, that you?"

"Yeah, Meg. Sorry to call so late, but I wanted to talk. I have so much to tell you."

"I don't care about the time. Tell me what's happening."

"Well, it's about my sister, Kate."

"She alright?"

"Sort of. It's so weird. Turns out she has the memories of the brain donor. She never told anyone because she was afraid the doctors would try to erase her memories again. I guess they were supposed to erase them, but they made a mistake."

Megan put her hand to her head. "Oh, whoa! What does she remember? Who was she?"

There was a brief pause as he cleared his throat. "When I asked, she acted strange, was really vague . . . like maybe she couldn't remember some of it. But now I understand so many things."

"What do you mean?"

"It was weird, back when she was eleven, maybe twelve-years-old, she would use these big words . . . words I had to look up in the dictionary to see what they meant. Seems the brain donor, whoever she was, was a college student. She remembered that much."

"God, maybe her parents are still alive. She probably even has brothers and sisters."

"Naw. She remembers that her mother died, and she thinks that either the father left them when she was really young or . . . well, maybe he died too. Something like that."

"That doesn't make sense. And why does she tell you all this stuff now? Why not back then?"

"Yeah. I asked the same thing. She says they . . . that is the doctors . . . are going to do another transplant soon, and this time it's some guy who's dying and they're gonna use another guy's body."

"Oh, jeez! They're gonna kill some other guy?"

"No. No. It's like a heart transplant. The other guy is brain dead, but they use the organ on a patient who is ill and will die without a transplant," he said, using his college training as an EMT.

That's another thing she liked about him. He was smart.

She relaxed, tried to let the information settle in. *At least it's not our problem.* "So we're okay?" she asked.

"Us? Sure. I gotta go to work tomorrow, but I'll see you next weekend. 'Kay? But Megan . . ."

"Yeah?"

"Don't tell anyone just yet, 'kay? My family wants to keep it on the down low for now."

"Sure, but why?"

"Just promise," he said, his voice pensive.

"Okay. But we'll still meet next Saturday? Same time, same plan?" she agreed, not caring as long as she could see Josh.

"Pick you up at 10:00, bright and early."

"G'night," she said.

She wondered how this news would change her relationship with Kate. But she was glad that his no-show wasn't because he wanted to dump her.

Chapter 25

Hope

Jamison sat back in the worn leather chair, a newspaper resting on his lap. He gripped the chair arms, swallowed, and watched Noah's reaction. The young man, dressed in ill-fitting blue jeans and a loose Aerosmith T-shirt sat slack-jawed for several seconds. All color drained from his gaunt face.

"I know you are aware that I once performed a brain transplant operation. But I wanted to discuss this with you before we speak to your parents, to be sure you understand the ramifications of what I'm telling you. As you know, eight years ago I performed a brain transplant and the patient is still alive." He held up the newspaper with the headline, "Brain Transplant Success."

He handed the newspaper to Noah, who scanned the headlines and searched Jamison's eyes for confirmation. Jamison scooted forward in his chair and briefly touched Noah's arm. "Back when I performed this surgery, I had no idea that the donor's memory was a necessary element in survival. Our team was erasing brain donor's memories with the belief that the body would revert back to its former identity. We performed four surgeries, and only one patient survived. Somehow our memory erasure procedure didn't take for that one. She retained the donor's memories. She kept it a secret from me for a year. Before I found out, I thought I'd been a failure. I'm still not over their deaths."

Noah nodded, clearly understanding at least somewhat the depth of his pain.

Jamison bent forward and pointed at Noah. "Look, you have a great mind, but what you need is a new body."

"Agreed," Noah said, his voice breathy from the disease.

Jamison sat back and closed his eyes for a moment until he had control of his emotions. He opened his eyes and said, "I believe it's possible for you to have a long and fruitful life. I'm betting on you."

Noah slumped back in his wheelchair and let out a long, loud sigh. For several seconds he sat stone still. Finally, he inhaled and stared at the newspaper. His eyebrows lifted. "It's really possible? You could give me a new body?"

Jamison felt a sudden release of tension. "Yes, Noah. But it won't be me that will do it. It'll be Dr. Johnson. She's now head of neurosurgery at Stanford. Just say the word, son, and we will speak to your parents. Then I'll fly you to California. Dr. Johnson believes that the hospital can do a search for a body donor—some young man who is brain dead but body healthy."

Noah trembled as he leaned forward, a faint smile appearing. It soon spread into a full-scale beam. A tear of joy trickled down his hollow cheek.

"I do. I do want to live!" Noah said, his voice choked. He wheeled his chair forward. "Tell me more. I need to understand what will happen, how long it will take to recover. I want to know everything . . . everything."

He became so animated and excited that he nearly fell out of his chair. Jamison stretched out an arm to catch him.

Noah's mother rushed into the room. "What's going on in here? What's all the commotion about?"

Noah grinned up at his mother. "Mum, the doctor says I can get a new body! Says it's possible."

Noah's mother frowned at Jamison. "What have you been telling my boy?"

If Noah could have stood up on his own, he would have danced. As it was, he wheeled his chair in circles and let out a loud "whoop."

He had resolved himself to an early death. Now, he had hope . . . hope that he might live another year . . . maybe even more.

Was it really possible? If he had a new body, what would he look like? Would he be strong? Would he be able to walk, run, skip? Could he do all the things that millions of other young men did? Or was it possible the illness would re-manifest itself? He would have a new body after all, with an entirely new set of genetics—genetics that didn't include cystic fibrosis. No, logic dictated that it shouldn't recur, he realized with a newfound joy that lit up his face in a smile that he couldn't contain.

Was it possible that some day a woman might love him? Could he ever become a father? Give his parents the thrill of being grandparents?

Noah looked at his mother through tear-soaked eyelashes. "Mum, take a read of this newspaper. Look at the headline," he said as he thrust it in front of her while pointing at the article. "Mum, I think God led Dr. Jamison here. I-I believe it." His voice cracked as he choked back a joyous sob. "You prayed for a miracle and . . . he knocked on our door," he said, indicating Jamison.

His mother's eyes grew wide as she studied the article. Noah could see that her hands were shaking.

"Is it truly possible?" she asked. "Can you do this?"

Noah saw Jamison nod at his mother. "I believe that it's possible. But there's much that needs to be done. It won't be easy and it *is* risky. We need to talk."

For the first time in his life, Noah felt giddy.

Maybe, just maybe, I can do all the things I always dreamed about.

Chapter 26

Some Body

Jamison's cell phone played "Rule Britannia." He flipped open his ancient cell phone and said, "Good morning."

"Dr. Jamison, this is Dr. Johnson."

"Dr. Johnson?" Jamison's mind jumped to the obvious conclusion. "Do you have news for me?"

"Yes, I think we have a donor. I'm not sure but—"

Jamison interrupted, "That's wonderful. I can't wait to tell Noah." *My God. My God, my prayers are answered.*

"Listen, Donald, the family wants to meet Noah first, before they agree to the surgery."

Jamison was so excited he stuttered. "A b-body donor? Tell me about the man. Tell me about the family." His hands trembled as he reached for a pad and pencil.

"His name is Kevin Whitehorse. He turned twenty-three on October twelfth and celebrated his birthday at a pub in Sacramento. It was Oktoberfest, and he drank a bit more than he should have," Johnson said.

"A car accident?" Jamison said as he jotted down the name and city.

"No. Not a car. It seems he enjoyed bicycling with his friends. He and his buddies rode to a restaurant in Old Sacramento and met up with Kevin's parents and sister. After the party, his friends said that they rode over to a park. Kevin was riding on a gravel shoulder and his bike slid off the side of the levy. He flew head over bike down a twelve-foot embankment and landed in the water. The current was swift and he was pulled under. Although he was rescued by one of his friends and was still alive, the lack of oxygen left him brain dead."

Jamison was excited but sad at the same time. He wasn't sure how to handle his emotions. He stopped taking notes. "How awful for his family, and on his birthday too."

"The bright spot here is that his parents have kept his body alive on machines for a little over two months, hoping for a miracle. They were about to pull the plug on the day that they got our notice."

Jamison closed his eyes to capture the moment.

It's meant to be.

"Here's the caveat. They're hoping that there is a chance that your Noah might care a little for them and they want to be sure that he is worthy of their son's body," Johnson said.

"That's not a problem. He's a jewel. You know what a tough old bird I am. If I like him, he's got to be exceptional."

Johnson laughed. "No kidding? Sounds like you've grown a heart in your old age."

Jamison smiled at the receiver, and then picked up the pencil again. "Hold on a sec. Let me check airline seating availability." He ran to his computer and found two seats for the next day's flight. He could get Noah and himself there, but not the family. Under the circumstances, he thought they would understand. "How soon can the donor family meet Noah? I can have him there by 1:30 in the afternoon two days from now."

"Based on Noah's records, I see why we need to move swiftly," Dr. Johnson said. "So, I'll call the family and will call you back with the date, time, and location for the meeting. Two days should be perfect."

"You're a wonderful doctor and a good person. Thank you." He put the pencil down again and scooted his chair back. "I'm going to go tell Noah . . . can't wait. When we arrive in the States, it will be Thanksgiving Day. And what a reason we have to be grateful, yes?"

Chapter 27

A Second Son

Noah felt helpless as Jamison removed the portable wheelchair from the rented van and helped him into it. Noah hated to admit it, but he had been growing weaker by the day, the flight taking its toll on both his health and stamina. He prayed that his appearance wouldn't tarnish the donor family's overall image of him.

Jamison laid an encouraging hand on his shoulder as they reached the front door of the modest home in Sacramento's Natomas area. Noah noted the fall foliage wreath on the door mixed with a few sprigs of holly. Although he missed Australia, he was eager for what lay ahead. As Jamison rang the bell, Noah listened and heard footsteps approaching. Hushed voices came from behind the door in what sounded like nervous conversation.

A tall, somewhat handsome, tanned man, whom Noah judged to be in his late forties or early fifties, opened the door. A middle-aged woman and teenager stood behind him. All three, dressed in what seemed to be their Sunday best, stared at him.

After a brief pause, the man said, "Hi! I'm Earl Whitehorse." He turned and motioned toward the two females. "And this is my wife Diana, and my daughter Aileen." Then he wiped his hand on his shirt and extended it to Jamison first.

"You must be Dr. Jamison," he said.

Earl gave Jamison what looked like a vice-grip handshake. Jamison winced as though it hurt.

"And you must be Noah Burnett," Earl, said, turning toward Noah with outstretched hand. Fortunately, when he took Noah's hand, the man was careful to be more gentle.

To demonstrate his resolve, Noah tried to stand up while grasping the tall man's hand.

"I'm so pleased to meet ya, Mr. Whitehorse, Mrs. Whitehorse, and Aileen." He stood for only a second or two, and then Earl and Jamison held onto him as he slumped, clumsily, back into the chair. Noah flushed, warm with embarrassment.

"Please, call me Earl," Mr. Whitehorse said. He frowned, looking uncomfortable, but quickly regained his composure. He opened the door wide and said, "Come in. Please."

Jamison had no trouble lifting the front wheels to navigate over the threshold since neither the chair nor Noah weighed much. Apparently Jamison had already warned the Whitehorse's about the wheelchair, Noah noted. Based on indentations in the carpeting, They had clearly moved some of their furnishings so that there was a wide pathway and a seating area that could accommodate him.

Noah looked around the room. It was a comfortable home, decorated in tones of mint green and dark wood with Native American artwork on the walls. The Thanksgiving table was decked out in a cornucopia of gourds and fall leaves with a smattering of orange and yellow mums. Noah's eyes went to the fireplace mantle and he stared at the many framed pictures of a young man with dark black hair, brown eyes, and a deep tan. In one, the man was with a young girl. They appeared to be on a hiking trip. In another he was wearing a baseball cap, smiling widely with his white, straight teeth that were impossible to miss. On his chiseled jaw was a scar—a small flaw that looked more like a trophy than a disfiguration. Three, four, five framed pictures with family and friends—a testament to the happy family unit they had once been.

Noah didn't wait for embarrassing starts. He took the lead. "I know how difficult this must be for ya. Please, feel free to ask me anything, anything at all. I want ya to know me, an' I want to know you too."

He looked at Diana, the mother. "What a grand young man your son, Kevin, must o' been. I can see from the photos on the mantle and wall that he was your pride, your joy. Ma'am, Sir, Aileen."

He lowered his eyes so that he wouldn't appear too brash. "If ya agree to take this journey with me, I promise to do everything I can to make ya proud of me. I know I can't take his place, but a part of your son, and a piece o' me, will simply share the same space. And I promise to honor you as a family, the family that gave me a chance to live a little longer and, maybe, to contribute something to society."

The mother's eyes grew moist and her lips trembled. She made a sad attempt at a smile, opened her mouth as if to speak, but then just nodded. She pulled a hand-embroidered hanky from her pocket and patted her eyes.

"What is it that you plan to do with your life, Noah?" Aileen asked.

Noah lifted his eyes to the young girl, the daughter. She was of medium height, her frame was solid and her voice had a singsong quality to it. Although the question was direct, her demeanor was that of someone kind and thoughtful, which offered a modicum of comfort. He spoke with as much force as his body could muster. "I've dreamed of being a doctor for as long as I can remember." He pointed at Jamison. "Not a brain surgeon like Dr. Jamison, but a family physician . . . I want to know the entire family, help them through the good and bad parts of life. I just want to serve."

Jamison stepped forward and said, "And I can tell you that the boy is a genius. He devours information, comes up with new solutions to old problems, and consistently beats me at chess."

Noah laughed. "Na' that's not true. We're tied. He likes to exaggerate a bit."

The father studied Noah for a moment and then said, "Dr. Johnson at Stanford has given us a lot of information about the procedure. It sounds very risky. Are there any assurances that this will work?"

Jamison started to speak, but Noah interjected. "None. But it's for certain that both your son and I teeter on the edge of life. We don't have much time left. This is the only hope for me *and* for yer son."

"Well," Earl said, his voice rasping with emotion, "perhaps we will have a Happy Thanksgiving after all. It's been tough finding any joy during this holiday season. But now, maybe we will have something to celebrate."

Chapter 28

Meeting of the Minds

Kate struggled with the idea of meeting with Noah. He was a stranger and the reason that her family, and eventually the world, would learn about her secrets. But he was a sick man, about to die.

She was told that he wanted to meet her, see how she had survived . . . a beacon of hope to a doomed man, as Jamison put it.

She straightened the collar on her blue cotton blouse and tried to brush the lint off her black woolen slacks. She fingered her gold-looped earrings.

Why am I so nervous?

The surgery was scheduled for the next morning.

One more day left to live, or to receive the gift of a long, healthy life. Which would it be?

It struck Kate that she hadn't had such a choice.

She stood for a moment outside the private room, but then stepped back as a man and woman came out. The man was tall, his features so striking that at first Kate thought he might have been a movie star. There was something powerful about this black-haired, black-eyed, dark-skinned man. She guessed he was Cherokee or maybe Osage. The woman was of medium height, which still put her three to four inches above Kate. She, too, had dark hair, but her eyes were light blue. There was an elegance about her. She walked as though her feet didn't touch the ground.

The couple stopped and the woman gave Kate a curious look. "Are you Kate, the girl who had the transplant?"

Kate's head snapped up. "Yes. I am. And you are?" she asked with one raised eyebrow.

"We're Kevin Whitehorse's parents." The woman lowered her eyes. "Noah will inherit our son's body." She motioned with her head toward the door. "We met with Noah the other day. He's a nice young man. We think he deserves a chance."

Kate wasn't sure what to say. "I-I'm glad that you agreed. I'm so sorry about your son."

Although the man towered over her, there was gentleness in his deportment. "If things work out, we know that a part of our son will still be with us." The tall man then angled his head toward her and added, "It's good that you're here." He opened the door and motioned for her to enter. "He told us that he's been expecting you."

Kate didn't hesitate. She forced a bright smile, wishing to offer Noah a hopeful image that he could take to the OR But when her eyes fell to Noah's frail, skeletal figure, she held back a gasp and automatically drew her hands into fists.

Tubes ran down his arms and electronic devices beeped. Kate couldn't look directly into his face because she was afraid she'd run. Instead, she stared at a point above his eyes.

"You're Kate, aren't ya?" he said with a deep but weak voice. "Dr. Jamison's miracle girl. Umm, sorry, not girl. You're obviously a woman."

Kate felt something melt inside her. Noah's voice didn't seem to match the infirmed man. "Yes, I'm Katherine Craig." She glanced briefly at the emaciated face.

He smiled, thin lips stretched across a withered canvass. "The great soprano. Dr. Jamison filled me in, and then I googled your name and watched some of your performances on YouTube. You are an amazing woman."

Kate sat carefully in the chair next to the bed trying desperately not to look as uncomfortable as she felt. "So, tomorrow will be the big day. I hear that you will have a powerful body when you wake up."

"Kevin Whitehorse's body, I can barely imagine. Ya know, before . . . oh, never mind. I don't want to talk about yesterday. But I do want to talk about tomorrow. Just the sight of you makes me optimistic. I truly believe that I will survive this. I want so very much to live a while longer."

"G-good. That's really good." She didn't know what to say to inspire him. Somehow she'd always found the right words, but today her mind was a blank. She motioned toward the door. "I met Kevin Whitehorse's parents as they were leaving. They seemed like nice people."

"Yeah, they are. Generous too."

Kate listened to the beeping of the monitors. They distracted her as she tried to think of something intelligent to say. "By the way, where is your family?"

"Ah, Mum and Da are still in Melbourne. Everything happened so fast that they couldn't get a flight, but I have called them and they are on the next flight out. They didn't want to slow us down once word came 'bout an available body." He winced. "That sounds so impersonal. I didn't mean it that way. But regarding my parents, by the time I am awake, when I'm 'renewed,' they should be here by then."

Kate looked up at the ceiling, wishing for advice from some friendly angel. "That's important. You'll need lots of support. And, you probably already know this, but it's your will to live and your memories that are going to keep you alive."

Now, as she lowered her head and peered directly into his eyes, he didn't seem as frail as he had at first. As a result of their short conversation and the passion that he displayed, she was convinced that he might very well survive. She looked at him again and saw something quite beautiful about him.

"I'll be here when you wake up," she said without thinking. "Yes, I'll be here and I'll pray for you, cheer for you. But you'll pull through even without me and my meager attempts. I can tell you're a winner."

"Live long and prosper," he said as he lifted a tube-ridden hand in the Spock gesture.

That line startled her, and she giggled despite herself.

"Even in Melbourne we get Star Trek," he said with a grin.

She stood and cocked her head sideways. "Well, then, nothing you say when I see you in a few days will surprise me." She touched his hand. "Rest, Mr. Noah. You have a big day ahead of you. As you know, Christmas is coming up soon and when you awake renewed, you'll get to experience a birthday in America with the baby Jesus."

She threw him a dimpled smile and walked from the room. As she exited, a tall, silver-haired man turned and grinned at her.

Her eyes went wide. "Dr. Jamison?"

"Thank you. Thank you," he said as he came to her side, threw his arms around her, and gave her a long, earnest hug. It was the last thing she had ever expected of this once distant man.

Something new was in the air.

"Happy Thanksgiving," he said.

Chapter 29

Two for One

Jamison, covered in a protective gown and facemask, watched the monitors and listened to the beeping as he sat next to Noah's bed. This was day two after the surgery. It had gone well, but there were so many things that could go wrong.

Just as he gently pulled the lightweight blanket up toward Noah's neck, he saw his young friend's eyes flutter. A moan came from Noah's new throat.

"He's coming to," Jamison told the ICU nurse. "Go tell Dr. Johnson."

He laid a hand on Noah's arm. "Noah, it's Donald, Donald Jamison. Son, you're going to be okay. You made it." He choked back tears. For too many years he'd missed the true miracle of the surgery that he'd performed eight years ago. Where both lives would have been lost, now at least one could be saved—an amalgam of two people. Kevin had been given a beautiful mind, and Noah, a beautiful body. It was the one silver lining from this terrible tragedy.

He thought of the Hippocratic oath: "Do no harm." No harm was done here. One life had been saved where none would have escaped death had the surgery not been performed. Jamison felt forgiven. The shame that had haunted him, when a young Kate had passed that note to him and he had realized that he had unknowingly sentenced three men to death by erasing their memories, was now expunged.

Noah's eyes opened. He looked dazed, confused. His pupils shifted from side to side, then focused on Jamison.

"Don't try to talk, Noah. Save your strength. I've already spoken to your parents. They're in the waiting room. They were up all night, so I told them to get a few minutes of shuteye—that I would call them when you woke up."

Jamison watched as Noah ran his tongue over his parched lips and looked down at his one unfettered hand. It was large, with long fingers. He lifted it in front of his face, turned the deep-tan hand palm facing him, then palm away. He clenched it into a fist, then opened it. He repeated the sequence several times. Then Jamison saw that an ever-so-small smile brightened the young man's face as his hand reached over to Jamison.

At that moment, Dr. Johnson entered the room. "So, our patient is awake."

"Get Mum and Da. And Kate. Where's Kate?" His eyes scanned the room. "She said she'd be here for the surgery. Is she?"

Jamison noted how different the boy's new voice was from his previous one. He still had that Aussie accent, but the tone was deeper, more sonorous than that of the pre-surgery Noah. It fit the body. It fit the man.

Dr. Johnson's eyebrows shot up and she looked at Noah with her head tilted to one side. "She's here, but only Dr. Jamison and family will be permitted in here until you are well enough to be moved."

"But she said . . ."

"Sorry, Noah. It'll have to wait," Dr. Johnson said.

Jamison stirred. "I'll let both your parents and Kate know that you're awake and that you asked for them. And if she has a message for you, I'll let you know." Then he bent down lower and said in a quiet tone, "I'll see if they can make an exception for Kate. I can't promise anything, but if I have any say, we'll get her in to see you." He winked.

Noah formed a faint smile, nodded, and then sank his bandaged head deep into the pillows. He closed his eyes and appeared to be asleep again within seconds.

Dr. Johnson nodded at Jamison as he left the room. In the hallway, he discarded the protective gown and mask, and then walked down the hall to the waiting area. As he entered, he saw that Noah's parents had been shunted aside as a woman shoved a microphone in Kate's face. Beside them both, a burly man was pointing a camera at Kate, who shook her head and said, "You're not supposed to be in the building. Please leave me alone."

Jamison rushed over and pushed the cameraman aside. "You know you're not allowed in here. Get out!" he shouted. "How did you get past security?" He hurried over to Kate's side and said, "Come with me. Quick." Then he added, "I'll be right back," to Noah's very groggy parents who had arrived in the wee hours of the morning. "Your son is awake. Give me just a minute with Kate, then he's all yours. I promise."

He saw the rush of relief on Noah's parents' faces as he took Kate by the hand and led her down the hall. Despite his plea for the woman and cameraman to leave, they continued to follow the pair, the woman shouting questions: "What was your name in your last life? Do you remember your family? How old were you when you died? Come on, Kate, everyone wants to know," the woman said.

"Security. Call security," Jamison said to a passing nurse. Jamison led Kate into an elevator, and pushed the button for the second floor. When the doors opened, he led her into a room that read, "Staff Only."

The room was quiet—empty except for a table and a few chairs while other chairs were stacked neatly in a corner. Watercolor paintings, one on each wall, hung mutely in the center of their respective spaces, each at exactly the same level. They were all landscapes, void of people or animals.

"Sorry about that, Kate. I knew this was going to be hard on you, but there was no other way."

Kate plunked down in one of the chairs and pulled it up to the table. "It's okay. I knew it would be like this, but I promised Noah that I'd be here." She pushed the dark curls off her forehead. "How come you won't let me in to see him?"

"Hospital rules," he said with a grimace. "I'll see what I can do to get you in soon. He's going to be okay . . . I think. Lots of tests and therapies, as you know."

Kate seemed to look intently at Jamison. "I just want him to know that I understand exactly what he's going through. He needs to see that I'm pulling for him."

Jamison let out a long breath. "Oh, Kate, he knows. Believe me, he knows. You were the first person besides his parents that he asked for when he awoke."

"Really?" she said as she forced another stray curl behind an ear. "Then you have to get me in to see him today. I have a performance tomorrow, and I can't miss it."

Jamison looked down and noticed his wrinkled shirt and trousers. He felt his face. Two days' worth of stubble had grown on his chin. He'd been with Noah's parents at his side, in the young man's room, since the surgery and had acted like an expectant father, pacing the floor. He'd watched the young man's every breath and had found himself taking in deeper breaths as though they would somehow influence Noah's breathing. He had even taken Noah's pulse every few minutes, though the monitor was measuring it.

Jamison nodded at Kate. "I'll go talk with Dr. Johnson again. Although she's a stickler for rules, she knows how much patient support is needed for the healing process. Maybe if she knows you have a performance later, she'll bend the rules. But you need to know that if she agrees, it may be just for a minute. Can you handle that?" With one eye nearly closed, he gauged her reaction.

"I understand," she said, frowning. "By the way, what does he look like now?"

Jamison steepled his hands. Then with a tender smile, he said, "Glad you asked. It's kind of shocking. He was so frail when you last saw him, and his features so very Australian. Now he's a six foot tall Native American with an Aussie accent. If he greets you with a 'G'day mate,' don't be surprised."

"I'd almost forgotten how different he might look, so I'm glad you reminded me. Sometimes I'm slow at putting two and two together."

"Well, the doctors put one and one together and got one fine-looking, fine-thinking young man. You might say that we got one for the price of two."

Kate grimaced at the gallows humor. "So Dr. Jamison, now you've developed a sense of humor too. Will wonders never cease?"

Jamison pursed his lips, gave a sudden nod. "Life experiences *do* change us, and you and Noah have changed me. I hope, for the better."

Fifteen minutes later, both Kate and Jamison were at Noah's side, gloved, gowned, and masked, their heads covered with caps.

"Noah, Kate's here," Jamison said.

Jamison noticed a visible shudder from the boy's tanned body as both of Noah's eyes slowly peeked open. Despite the several small tubes invading his body and nasal passage, one corner of his face turned upward.

"K-Kate. You're here."

"I told you I'd be here. I always keep my word."

She had been told that she couldn't touch him, but from a few feet back, she raised a gloved hand, waved, and blew him a kiss. "Christmas will be here soon, Noah. And with it, you will have been given the gift of life. There is no greater gift."

Noah nodded.

They spoke with the young man for a few minutes longer. Then they stopped on their way out so that Jamison could let the two families know that Noah was able to take visitors, but not to tire him out too much. He needed his rest if he were to regain strength.

When Jamison and Kate left the building, hats on and heads down to disguise themselves, Jamison peered up slightly and noticed that the protesters were chanting against the transplant surgery just as they had been eight years ago. But there weren't as many protesters this time around, and the wind had been taken out of their sails once they learned that the surgery had been a success and that both the brain donor and body donor's families were celebrating the outcome.

It's hard to rail against life, Jamison thought as he exited, tired but happy. *Life is the winner here.*

Chapter 30

Spring Is in the Air

Megan chewed on the eraser of the No. 2 pencil as she thought about what to write. She wanted to put her words on paper first, make sure her message was perfect. Then she could finger it into a text and send it off to Josh. She looked at what she had written, tore the page from the pad, wadded it up and tossed it into the can. She started again: "Hey BF . . ."

Her spirits had always echoed the seasons. The short, dark days of winter usually brought about a sense of sadness and a desire to stay in bed. She called it her hibernation syndrome. But then, as spring approached, she would normally grow increasingly cheerful, but not this year. Things were topsy-turvy. Her winter days with Josh and Kate had been a high point, but now, as spring approached, she felt sad because Kate was less available to her. For the next few months she would be on the road, performing in various cities. To make things worse, Josh had returned to the University of Oregon for the spring quarter. It would be months before she would see him again. It was important that she write something that would keep him interested.

She looked at the books on her desk and pushed them aside. Plenty of homework still to do, but the text was her priority.

A message ding on her smartphone got her immediate attention. *Maybe from Josh.* But no, it was her friend Emily.

Next weekend is my family's last
ski trip to Tahoe. Wanna go?
Fresh snow.

Megan dropped the pencil and responded:

I'll ask my fam.

She threw a T-shirt over her bra, stepped into a pair of jeans, and ran barefooted to the living room. Not only did she love to ski, but Emily's family had a really chic two-bedroom timeshare, and Emily was fun to be with.

Megan was almost breathless when she got to the foot of the couch. "Mom, Dad, Emily has asked if I want to go skiing next weekend with her family. Can I? Please, please, pleaaase say yes. I'm working on my homework and I'll have everything finished. I promise."

Her father gave her a stern look. "What about your chores? You are supposed to feed and walk Algae this week."

"No problem. I'll ask Mark to trade with me." She looked at her mom, trying not to appear too anxious, worried they might not approve if she seemed overly eager.

Her dad glanced over at her mom. "What do you think, Marcy?"

"Well, I don't know. This is rather sudden, isn't it? Are you sure that her parents invited you, or is this just something that Emily thinks they might approve if she asks?"

"And what about the cost?" her dad added. "Do you have the funds to rent the equipment and to pay for the lift fee?"

"I have the money, and I'm sure her parents suggested it. They really like me. They said so when I went with them last November . . . said I was good with Emily. Oh, please say yes."

Her dad sat back in his chair and cupped his chin. "Go in the other room and let us think about it. Ask us again in the morning. And if you really want to go, do your homework."

Megan fidgeted. "I think they want to know now. It's just a few days away. If I don't get back to her, she might invite someone else. Please?"

Her father shook his head but then took a deep breath. "Well, okay," he said. "But I want to verify this with her parents. If they say you're invited, then you can go."

He gave her a strange smile that didn't seem to go with the words, but she didn't care. She figured it probably had something to do with Josh. She knew he didn't want her seeing him, though she wasn't sure why. He was studying for a career and was polite to her parents. Still, the fact that she wouldn't be able to see him next weekend might help in their decision.

"What's their number? I'll call them now," Bruce said.

"Just a minute. I'll get it."

Megan ran back to her room and came back with her cell phone. She searched contacts and gave him the number as he entered it into the digital phone.

After introductions, he said, "Say, my daughter, Megan, just got a text from Emily inviting her to Tahoe next weekend. I just wanted to touch bases with you to see if you were aware of the offer. Oh, good. We just wanted to make sure that you approved. Yes, she can go. And thank you for inviting her."

When her dad was through with the conversation and gave her his approval, she skipped back to her bedroom and texted her acceptance to Emily. Then she went to her closet and looked at her warm winter outfits to decide what she should wear. Maybe she needed a new faux fur-lined jacket. It was the end of the season, so coats and jackets would be on sale. *Turquoise, that's the best color on me. I'll find a coat at Macy's tomorrow.*

Hopefully, her appearance on the slopes would be in good taste, especially in the lodge. Hot cider and a warm fire in the mammoth fireplace after a day on the slopes was one of her favorite pastimes. Yes, she was going to be killin' it!

Early spring, what a wonderful time of the year!

Bruce knew his daughter, Megan, very well. She was flighty, impetuous, and somewhat unreliable. He hoped that the outing with Emily would give Megan a chance to meet other young men. Maybe she would find someone more fascinating than Josh.

Bruce looked at his wife. "You thinking what I'm thinking?"

Marcy shrugged. "Who knows? Some girls go steady with a dozen boys before they get serious. Maybe, just maybe, she'll play the field. I sure hope so."

Chapter 31

Lovelorn

Megan picked up her cell phone, then scanned the saved emails and text messages from Josh. Summer had come too slowly for Megan's liking, her thoughts continually drifting to Josh. Still, school would soon be out, and the two of them were already making plans to spend the best part of the summer together. Her parents hadn't been happy when she picked up her relationship with Josh right where she left off. She knew what they were up to, letting her go on that ski trip. They had hoped she would find someone new, forget about Josh, but she hadn't, she realized with a smile.

Now she and Josh were texting or communicating every day. She was glad they had the same phone provider so the minutes didn't cost a bundle.

Megan threw herself onto her bed and dreamed of next week. She couldn't wait to see him. Her best friends knew everything about him. She even wore the University of Oregon Duck promo shirts and caps to her hometown sporting events just to emphasize that she was going with a college dude . . . and to drive her parents batty. Not only that, but Kate kept in touch by text during her tours—one more thing that drove her parents batty.

She rolled onto her back. Next month she would turn eighteen and she'd be an adult, able to make her own decisions regardless of what her parents said.

She sent him her third text of the morning:

Can't w8 2 c u. <3 <3 <3

Ditto

Megan smiled, hopped off the bed, and ogled the framed picture of Josh. This was the last week of school and graduation ceremonies would take place on Thursday. Just then her phone chimed a text. It was from her friend, Zach.

Go 2 Sr bash with me?

Zach was a tall blond senior in her chem class. He was brilliant. At least that's what he told her, and she believed him, especially since both of them were getting an A in the course.

Zach had always been at her elbow, pointing at the right answers, kidding her ever so gently when she messed up. At first she didn't even like him. And although he always smiled at her, she had interpreted his posture and tone as arrogance. But as time passed, she found him to be okay. His brown eyes sparkled and danced with each new discovery.

Unlike most guys, he was talkative and much of what he rambled on about was miles over her head. All she could do was nod and pretend she understood. Because of her brain-void, she became determined to stay on level with him, so during the past months she had thrown herself into studying science and mathematics in a way she had never applied herself before. Soon science, technology, and inventiveness had become her other passions. It was the broad vista of discoveries that captured her energy. Zach was nice as a lab partner, but she hadn't thought of him as anything more.

Megan hadn't planned to go to the senior dance because . . . well, Josh was her guy. But it could be fun. It wouldn't mean anything.

I'm sure Josh would understand that Zach is just a friend.

Maybe not. She decided to call him and see what he said. She lifted the phone to her mouth and said, "Call Josh's cell phone."

Ten minutes later, Megan grinned ear to ear, said a long, moony goodbye to Josh, and ran from the bedroom to the kitchen. Her parents were seated at the table eating dinner.

"Mom, Dad, my friend Zach wants me to go to the senior prom with him. I'm so excited!" she squealed. "What do you think?"

They both dropped their spoons and a small smile creased the sides of her dad's mouth.

"How wonderful," her mom said, a smudge of chocolate dripping from her lower lip. "I'm sure you'll have a good time." She wiped her lip with the back of her hand. "Guess we need to go shopping for a new dress, huh?"

"Oh, yeah," Megan chirped.

Her dad just smiled and nodded.

Megan thought she saw a tear form in her dad's eyes. But he ran a finger across the lids. "Cookie dough," he said. His voice seemed choked, like something had gone down the wrong pipe.

For a moment she found their smiles troublesome. She felt confused: first Josh said to go for it, and now her parents looked way too happy for this new twist. *Are they really that set on me not dating Josh?*

Before that thought began to deepen her suspicions, her father redeemed himself by saying, "We want to meet this guy." In typical fatherly fashion, he lifted a brow and added, "Although you've mentioned his name once or twice, we have never met him and we want to make sure he's worthy."

A surge of relief rushed through Megan, but she gave them the look of exasperation that only a teenager can give, and then followed it with the okay sign. "I'll tell him that he has to come by and get your approval, or should I say blessing?" She added her favorite teen tone to the word *blessing*.

"Approval will do," her mom said with a wink.

Megan skipped back to her room as she texted back.

Sure :-)

Chapter 32

Noah's Arc

Noah used a paper towel to dry himself under his armpits and applied more deodorant. He couldn't remember ever being so nervous. Even the transplant surgery hadn't caused this much anxiety.

Then Noah walked over to the window of his hospital room and took a final glance at the view. He recalled the agonizing days of physical therapy, the countless walks in the gardens with his parents and Kevin Whitehorse's parents.

Now they are my second family.

He recollected the efforts his parents had to make to accept his new persona. They kept trying to help him even after he was quite able to fend for himself. For so many years they had been his caregivers. Now he realized that someday he would be able to repay their attentiveness by caring for them . . . when the time came.

He thought about the nurses and Dr. Johnson. So many memories were indelibly etched in his mind. For a fleeting moment he wondered if he could actually exist outside of the hospital domain. A dark thought hit him, *so far so good, but there is still a chance of organ rejection.* He knew that his daily regimen of drugs and therapies would continue, probably for the rest of his life, just as they had for Kate.

He glanced down past his barrel chest to his size 11½ shoes. Even before his illness, he had never been very big. Now he was six feet tall and gaining weight. In his old body he'd been twenty-six years old. Now he was twenty-three.

He still had an Aussie accent, but the words formed differently in his mouth so that they came out slightly unique. He supposed that only he would notice the difference.

His mind was reeling from all the changes as he leaned against the windowsill and inhaled deeply. The sun was out and light rain was falling. A multicolored arc washed across the panorama—a rainbow.

A sign from above? Noah's Arc?

Those thoughts brought a grin to his face. Doubt was shed like a worn-out jacket.

He heard a knock on the hospital door, and before he could answer, Jamison walked in.

"Well, today is the big day," Jamison said as he entered Noah's hospital room. Jamison was dressed in a bright red cardigan, white collar and cuffs peeking out from underneath it, and a pair of gray trousers to finish off the look. "Are you ready to move out of this place?" he asked.

Noah was already fully dressed in one of his new outfits that the Whitehorses had bought for him. He thought that he looked somewhat dashing in his black jeans, orange and black 49er polo shirt, and black tennies. Jamison watched as Noah looked in the bathroom mirror, moved a comb through his short black hair, and wondered at his transformation. Noah had heard of out-of-body experiences, but could see that this was quite the opposite. Getting accustomed to his new body seemed to be downright wonderful, but also weird.

"You okay?" Jamison asked.

Noah merely nodded and said, "Even six months after the surgery, when I dream at night, I see myself as the thin, brown-haired Australian. And when I awaken each morning it's as though I have just been jettisoned into a new life. I wonder just how long it will take for my brain to fully register my new physical self?"

Jamison said, "Give it time, son. Kate says it will come but that it takes some time."

Noah walked over to Jamison. "I am so ready, thanks to you and Kate. So it's off to Sacramento."

Jamison placed his hands on Noah's shoulders and grinned a sly grin. "Your parents and the Craig family, including that little Miss Kate, are waiting to celebrate your success. They're all over at the Whitehorse residence. Lots of media outside the hospital, though, and I'm sure that they will follow us to Sacramento. You ready for that?"

Noah heard footsteps approaching and he turned in time to see Jamison's wife, Inna, enter the hospital room. She ran over to him and gave him a friendly hug. "My dear Noah, there's no way that I could miss this occasion," she said, and then offered him a look of profound joy.

Noah marveled at Inna. She had the good looks and deportment of a beautiful, mature beauty queen. Everything about her echoed the word *class*.

"Ah, Mrs. Jamison, I'm glad that ya are here. I wasn't expecting ya!" He beckoned her toward him. "Ya know, you are partly responsible for my transformation—to my new life. If it hadn't a been for your neighborliness, meeting me and my parents, and urging your husband ta meet with me and play a game o' chess wid me, well—you know, I'd be dead now."

Inna gave him a second hug. "Look at you. You are absolutely gorgeous." Then she stepped back as if to analyze him.

"Thanks," he said, feeling shy suddenly.

"But listen here, young man, don't let that beautiful body of yours, or your celebrity status, take you off course. We expect you to follow through with becoming a doctor. Remember?"

"Do I remember? Thanks ta your husband, I have a scholarship ta the University of California at Davis, an' I take it very seriously."

Inna beamed at her husband with pride. Then she turned her attention back to Noah. "We are both so very proud of you." She touched his arm. "You provide hope to thousands of others. It's wonderful."

Jamison strode over and put an arm around his wife's slender waist. "My wife's right," he said with a smile, ". . . as usual." He gave his wife a special look and added, "But seriously, Noah, although you are only the second successful brain transplant, you won't be the last. The excitement over your recovery has been heralded around the world. Cases are already lining up. So my dear Noah, stay well. Take care of yourself."

"You are laying a lot of responsibility on me, but I take it willingly. God bless ya." He took both their hands and gave them each a squeeze, then he walked over to the hospital bed to prepare for the trip home.

Noah opened his suitcase and checked it over for the third time in twenty minutes. The contents included the following items: toothbrush, prescriptions, slippers, PJs, letters from UC Davis, clothing, underwear, socks, shaving gear, and floss.

"I think you're ready for the journey," Jamison said.

"Aye, I'm ready to go," he said as he zipped up his suitcase and picked it up as though it weighed nothing. He marveled at his newfound strength.

"Lead on, old grand wizard," Noah said as he linked arms with Jamison and Jamison linked arms with Inna.

"Whadaya mean, old?" Jamison said. "I'm in my prime."

Chapter 33

Questions

Noah couldn't believe how big the UC Davis campus felt after so many years confined to a wheelchair. Neither could he get over how good it felt to be walking upright again on two legs.

"Hi, Noah!" one of the campus coeds called to him, flipping her long black hair and giving him her most sultry look.

"G'day," he replied, glancing at her and then looking quickly away.

When had he gone from a person that everyone looked on with pity to a heartthrob? It felt strange. Made him uncomfortable and yet flattered. After all, it wasn't *his* body that they were attracted to. It was Kevin Whitehorse's. If the women had known him—the *real* him—would they be so flirtatious? Only Kate had known and accepted the real him. She'd liked him in both bodies. He smiled at the thought, wishing she would text him.

They had texted, skyped, and emailed back and forth ever since his operation. It was the hope of hearing from her that had kept him going in those horrible months following the surgery. That and the occasional visit to his hospital room. He knew she was busy, always on the road, but he held out hope that she wouldn't forget him despite her busy schedule.

He heard a ping and fumbled for his phone, scrolling down to see who had contacted him. It was Jamison. He found a bench and took a seat next to the commons.

How's college? Your parents are well. Trying to keep the journalists at bay. How about U?

Noah bent over, fumbling, his fingers feeling awkward still, as though they belonged on some other hand.

Same here. Getting pretty good at outwitting them. Uh-oh—speak of . . . gotta run!

Across the green, a pair was headed his way. He could tell they were journalists by the pancake makeup and the camera bag. Thank god for chess. Time for this knight to head west.

The London sky was dark, gray, and foreboding. Kate placed her cup of tea on the side table, wrapped her soft bamboo robe around herself, and sat on the couch. She sank into the buttery soft leather sofa and curled her legs over onto the adjacent cushion. It was the only way she could get comfortable. If she sat like a "lady" with her back against the couch and her legs in front, she was so short that her legs would dangle. She so wished she had been three or four inches taller as she'd been in her previous life.

Guess I can't have everything!

She let out a long sigh, picked up the cup, and sipped the steaming Earl Grey tea, inhaling the sweet aroma. Heaven.

In deference to Bruce and Marcy's feelings about Josh and Megan, Kate had tried to make her text messages to the pair sound so-so. Little by little she wanted Megan to know some of Josh's faults. She pointed them out in jest—like his stinky feet, and she kidded about his macho ways, hoping that a wise girl of today would see this as a flaw. But it wasn't just the Megan/Josh situation that bothered her. It was Gino too.

She closed her eyes and could still feel Gino's caresses even though he left for Italy yesterday. She'd hated herself for succumbing to his advances, but she had been a wife once, and she knew what it was to be with a man. This nomadic life gave her no chance to meet anyone. She touched her lips and could still summon the feel of his kisses. Was it love or simple need? She knew the answer, and yet she wanted more, from the right man if he were out there. For some odd reason, her thoughts turned to Noah. She'd seen him only a few times over the past few months, but they texted or skyped regularly. Of all the people she had known since her surgery, he was the one who understood her most, what she had been through, how lonely it could be in another person's body—in another person's life.

She swirled the tea, took another sip and let it linger on the back of her palate, her thoughts turning to the past. She remembered how reckless she had been at nineteen . . . almost two decades ago when she was Liz. Her recent relationship with Gino, if she could call it that, felt just as reckless. Maybe it was just his beautiful voice and how he serenaded her that had her in a trance—like all the other young female fans that drooled over him when he sang. He was handsome. He had told her she was the "lucky" one. But was she? He had finally told her that he loved her, but the words came as he was trying to seduce her. She ran her finger around the rim of her cup, thinking.

For months they had traveled together, being paired as "the most romantic couple in opera." They had flown around the globe, performing in one opera house after another. Now they would be separated for months, Gino with his televised performances in Italy, and she with contracts in London, Paris, and Vienna. She was almost relieved for the time apart.

She had tried to let him know that she cared for him as a friend, but he had said bitter things when she pushed him away—called her a tease, said that he was "disappointed" in her. Worse yet, he had acted like a spoiled child who had been denied a piece of candy. He'd had the audacity to pout.

Kate stood up, laid down the cup and walked around the hotel suite. She needed to get him out of her thoughts and concentrate on her upcoming performances. The two of them wouldn't be performing together again for the rest of the year. They would be in the same vicinity possibly three or four times in the coming year. That would give her time to reflect on their relationship, if there was such a thing, and to decide how best to handle it. The rest of the time they would text and have long-distance conversations. She just hoped that if he truly did love her, as he said he did, he would have time to grow up—to show it through his actions.

Funny how she didn't look forward to Gino's messages the way she did Noah's. She picked up her cell phone. Maybe she could send him a quick text before her next performance.

Chapter 34

Half Empty Nest

Bruce paced the floor. Marcy's, Kate's, and his hopes that Megan's infatuation with Josh would fizzle didn't happen. Even though Megan had a nice time with Zach at the senior dance, it had amounted to nothing more. She had rejected the young man's other requests. Now Megan was eighteen, and Josh was twenty-four. Josh would be finishing his master's in December. Worse yet, they were talking marriage plans for the following June.

I can't let that happen.

"I think the girls are ready," said Marcy. "The car is packed to the brim with their belongings. It's time to take them to their dorms."

Bruce looked at his daughters and felt an emptiness. Both were leaving home and entering San Jose State. Adrianna would be studying for an elementary teacher's credential while Megan, like her birth mother, would be studying marketing. The similarities between Liz and Megan were undeniable. She looked, thought, and behaved just like Liz had at that age. That's what caused him the most distress. *She's just like her mother.*

Bruce's head was spinning. At the same time, Mark and Shaun were ecstatic that their sisters were departing and they now would each have their own bedrooms—and no more drama.

"Bye bye," Mark hollered. "We'll miss you—NOT. Ha ha. See you in the next century."

"Yeah, so long you guys," Shaun waved.

"Well, we won't miss them either," Megan whispered to Adriana, though Bruce felt certain that both sets of kids were covering how they really felt.

Bruce turned to Marcy and watched as she gave both girls a hug while trying to hide her tears. She gave them a smile and words of encouragement. Then she shook her finger at the boys. "You think this is funny. But mark my word, you will miss them too."

Bruce circled his shoulders to get some much needed relief. "Okay, we're off. I'll be back before dinner, as soon as I get these two settled in."

Marcy gave him a wistful look and ordered the boys back into the house.

Bruce felt like an arm had been cut off. For some reason he had put the eventuality of this day out of mind. But the day had come anyway. Megan and Adriana were adults now in every sense of the law. They could vote. They could marry. They could even join the Army. What burned him was that the pair were leaving his nest where he could protect them, keep them safe. No more, "As long as you live in my house, you do as I say." They were adults who would face the dangers of the world on their own, and that thought gave him pause.

"You have everything?" he asked.

"Yes, Dad, we have our schedules, the list of books we need to buy, clothes, and our supplies. Remember, you helped us make a list and check it off."

"Okay. I just don't want to have to make another trip to the campus to bring you something you've forgotten."

But that wasn't what was really bothering him. Josh would be less than seven hours away, working on his own degree. Soon he would have a career and be ready to settle down with Megan.

Then Bruce, Marcy, and Kate would have to tell them the truth. Wouldn't they?

Chapter 35

Being Noah

Noah stared at his laptop screen and was wowed at the power of Facebook. He tapped the icon for friends. He had accepted well over 3,000 requests and only nine had he initiated: his birth parents; his adopted Whitehorse parents and sister, Aileen; Dr. Jamison and Inna; Dr. Johnson; and Kate. The rest were requests from around the world with many from his home country and hundreds from China, India, and Europe. But his number one friend, the one he queried and responded to most often, was Kate. He followed her performances, commented on them, and felt a special thrill whenever she wrote something on his postings.

Despite all the new friends, he still felt lonely, as though he were living a lie in someone else's skin. When people met him, he wondered if they liked him for who he was or for his outward appearance.

Still, he felt more than lucky. Blessed even. Now he had two families: his Australian Burnett family and the donor Whitehorse family, where he lived while attending UC Davis. And then there was Kate. He looked forward to the conversations and messages that he and Kate exchanged. She was so supportive . . . and so kind. Three times she had visited him during his recovery, always there with a smile and encouragement. The last time he'd seen her, she told him that he was in her prayers and had given him a kiss on the forehead. That had sustained him through the trial of recovery.

He picked up the birthday card that Kate had sent him in celebration of the one-year anniversary of his surgery. The message was handwritten, so different from the several ecards he'd received from friends and admirers. Despite her busy schedule, she had taken the time to sit down and put her hand to paper. He'd reread it every day since receiving it.

Dear Noah,

I am so proud of you and your achievements. Word is that you are one of the top students at UC Davis. I'm confident that someday you will be a great doctor. How wonderful that your Whitehorse family had a spare room for you while attending Davis. Just think, there are now eight others like us . . . brain-transplant survivors. We are part of a unique club. I feel a special kinship with each of them. Life is so precious.

P.S. I just wanted you to know that I'll be performing in your birth country at the Sydney Opera house in six weeks. I will be Pamina in Mozart's The Magic Flute. I wish you could be there to hear it. But I know that's not likely.

Do have a wonderful birthday and celebrate the miracle.

Yours truly,

Kate

Noah looked up the dates of the performance. *Wintertime here, summertime there—and she'll be there, singing at the famous Sydney Opera House during my semester break.*

He had thought about spending the two weeks with his parents in Melbourne, but the expense had seemed daunting. Now he reconsidered. He missed his mum and da and the thought of watching Kate perform thrilled him. Just seeing her again would make him feel less lonely.

He googled flights. The cheapest round trip was over $2,200 with stopovers. It would take more than thirty hours. He booked it, paid with a credit card, and placed a long-distance call.

"Mum, it's me, Noah. . . . Yes, I know, sorry to reverse the charges, but I've just spent my last dime on a round-trip ticket to come home for the holidays. . . . Yes I'll send ya an email with the particulars. Can't wait to see you both."

He said his goodbyes, hung up and walked over to the mirror. He looked at his tall sturdy frame, the dark tone of his skin, the scar on his chin, and the straight Roman style nose.

I wonder if Kate will recognize me.

His hair had grown thick and covered the thin scar at his scalp line. He laughed. He hadn't thought of it before today, but now he was in the body of a Native American whereas when he awoke from the surgery a year ago he had looked as though he'd been scalped.

Should I text Kate? Let her know that I'll be there? No, I'll surprise her . . . make it a special moment.

Chapter 36

The Galah

Kate sat at her dressing table reliving the five-minute standing ovation and multiple curtain calls that she and the cast had just experienced. Although the rehearsals were exhausting, the thrill of the performance always invigorated her.

Kate's manager, Cassie, knocked twice, then burst into her dressing room. As always, she was dressed in purple, and her skirt was just the right length to show off her long, pretty legs.

"You were magnificent, again. So many curtain calls," she said as she handed Kate an enormous vase filled with white cymbidium orchids. "From an admirer."

Kate stared at the vase. "Oh heavens, the room is already full of flowers."

"I guess they don't know that the heavy fragrances of some of these bouquets irritate your throat," her manager said with a laugh.

"You're right. They're not good for my voice," Kate said, sneezing.

"Ah, but these are special." Cassie handed a card to Kate. "The admirer told me that these orchids are not just beautiful but are guaranteed to be allergen-free."

"Well, that was thoughtful. Then I'll enjoy these." Kate pried open the envelope and, before withdrawing the card, gestured to Cassie and said, "You know what to do with the other floral arrangements."

"Yeah, donate them to the nearest hospital for long-term patients. Ones with few or no visitors."

Kate read the card and, seeing the name at the bottom, jumped up from her chair. "He's here! He's here! These are from Gino. I knew he'd be coming, but I didn't think he'd be here this soon."

Kate still didn't know how she felt about Gino. She just knew she was happy to see someone other than a fan. They were wonderful, but it wasn't the same as having a friend, and Noah promised to be a no-show, what with school and the cost of travel. She understood, though she had to admit she was more than a little disappointed. He was one of the rare people who understood what it was like to be a brain-transplant survivor—the conflicting emotions of gratitude and loss and he loneliness of living in another person's skin. But at least she would have Gino to keep her company while she was here.

"He's waiting right outside," Cassie said with a wink.

"Why didn't you tell me right away?" Kate stood and unzipped the back of her outfit. "Help me get out of this costume and into my street clothes. I haven't seen him in four months."

Cassie rolled her eyes and gave Kate a hand. "Don't I know it."

As soon as the costume fell to the floor, Kate set to work trying to wipe off the heavy makeup and rearrange her hair. In a matter of minutes, she was put together. She took one more quick glance in the mirror, shrugged, and looked over at Cassie.

"What do you think?" she asked.

"Adorable. Go on. Get out of here and have a good time."

Kate took a moment to gather herself so that she wouldn't look too anxious, and then opened the door. She saw Gino leaning against the wall adjacent to her.

"Ah, *mi amore*," he said when he saw her. He pulled her over to him and lifted her chin, planting a lingering kiss. Kate's head swam. It felt like a lifetime since she had felt a man's arms around her. Even now, she could feel the muscles in his arms as they tightened around her waist. His breathing became heavy, but then she noted the acrid smell of liquor on his breath. That was another thing about Gino—he liked to drink. She opened her eyes, gently pushed him away, and noticed another man standing across the way. She took a second look. Something about him seemed vaguely familiar.

Gino turned, saw the man too and said, "You got a problem, *Signore*? Kate's not giving interviews right now. Come back next week."

Noah stepped forward so that the overhead lights revealed his face, the scar on his chin and the two fresh yellow roses in his hand.

Kate gasped. "Noah, is that you?"

Before she could rush to him, Gino grabbed her arms and turned her abruptly toward himself. "How do you know this man?" he said in an angry voice, one full of accusation.

Kate pulled away. "Chill out, Gino. This is Noah. He's the second transplant survivor and my Facebook friend." She loosened Gino's grip on her and walked over to Noah and threw her arms around him in a giant hug.

"You came. I didn't think you would be able to get away." She heard Gino grunt and mutter something in Italian. Kate leaned back to get a better look at Noah, and then fingered his dark hair. "And look at your hair. It's so thick. You look great. How do you feel?"

"I'm fine," Noah said, looking past her to Gino. "But I'm sorry, I dinna mean ta interrupt you two. Jus wanted to offer my congratulations. You were a fantastic Pamina." He held out the yellow roses to Kate.

She thanked him, and then took the flowers and paused.

"I'm off to see my parents and Dr. and Mrs. Jamison in Melbourne. This was a stopover, so I thought I'd see you. . . . Catch the opera on my way home."

"Don't go," Kate said. "Come out with us." She turned and looked at Gino, pleading. "You don't mind, do you? This is such a surprise, both of you on the same day. There's so much to catch up on."

Gino threw out his arms and gave her an incredulous look. "But, *mi amore*, I have made reservations for us . . . just the two of us . . . at the Farmhouse King's Cross Restaurant."

Noah blinked rapidly, as if to hide his embarrassment. "No. No. You two go on. I've already eaten." With downcast eyes he added, "I need to be on my way . . . gotta catch a plane tonight."

That settled, Gino walked over to Noah and shook his hand. "So nice to meet you. Maybe we will see you again some time, *non*? *Arrivederci*."

"Ya. G'day mate. You are a real *galah*."

"Thank you so much for coming, Noah. And thanks for the roses. They're lovely. Please keep in touch," she added, giving his hand one last squeeze. "Promise."

He stared after her, wishing she could run to him as he walked a few steps away. As a student on scholarship—and not well-financed—it had cost him a lot to be here today. But he couldn't very well come between them.

"Come on, *mi amore*," he heard Gino say, taking her by the elbow. "I have a limo waiting for us. Your manager was wonderful in setting up this evening. It will be *fantastico*. And besides, I want you all to myself."

Kate looked over at Noah, her face red with embarrassment. "Okay, Gino. But first let me ask Cassie to put these roses in water."

Noah realized that Gino didn't know that he was still watching and listening. Gino smirked and reached for the roses. "Two little flowers? Give them to me and I'll toss them. They are not good for the voice."

Kate drew back. "No. It was a kind *gift*. Yellow roses are the symbol of friendship."

Noah overheard Gino's next comments very clearly. "Not friendship," amended Gino. "He looked at you with desire. He doesn't want you as an *amicoa*. I know. I can tell."

Noah realized that Gino was right. He did want more from Kate.

Kate pushed away from Gino.

"You behaved badly. He's a good friend who's been through a terrible ordeal."

Gino's brow wrinkled. "Kate, what's a *galah*?"

She shrugged as she entered the dressing room. "I dunno. Maybe it's Aussie slang for gentleman."

Noah snickered under his breath.

Chapter 37

Not Good Enough for Her

Noah sat at the airport terminal tapping his fingers noisily on the armrest. He stopped for a moment and looked at his long fingers and large hands. He still had moments when he thought of himself in his old body. But the instances were becoming less and less prevalent. He was one of the lucky few—one of the survivors. If it hadn't been for Jamison and Kate, he would have died months ago.

He stretched his cramping fingers, then leaned back in his chair. The overseas flight had been one of anticipation. He was still on heavy medications and his health was being monitored for possible organ rejection. Nonetheless, during the long hours and stopovers, he had practiced what he would say to Kate. But then his dreams had evaporated into dust the moment he saw that vile man kiss her.

What a fool I've been.

He found that he was grinding his teeth again, something he did, even in his old body, when he was upset. Should he tell Kate what he had seen before the opera had ended? He had caught the man kissing one of the women from the cast while offstage. Then the cad had the gall to meet with Kate as though none of that had ever happened, treating her like a possession. He let out a deep breath to relieve his stress.

If he didn't tell her what he'd seen, what kind of a friend would he be? She was the reason he was alive today. It disgusted and angered him that the bloody bloke could be so unfaithful to Kate. She deserved so much better.

When Noah had heard the man make coarse remarks to every pretty girl that had walked by him backstage, he hadn't known that he was Kate's beau. He had even seen the bounder whisper something into one blonde girl's ear, who then wrote something onto a slip of paper and gave it to him.

Was it any of his business? Should he just ignore what he saw? He had so much more on his mind—his studies, his finances, his parents and all that he owed to doctors Jamison and Johnson. But Kate had been there for him when he faced that surgery. She was a woman of her word. He owed her.

I've got to tell her, but at the right time, in the right way. His mum was wise in the ways of women. He would ask her what to do.

He was jerked from his thoughts when the flight personnel called for boarding. He shifted his focus to what he knew would be a warm welcome by his parents and good neighbors. Perhaps he would ask Dr. Jamison for his advice if he had some personal time with him.

He felt certain that friends and family had daily plans for him during the short time he'd be there. He pulled out his cell phone, swiped it open and pushed the speaker button, "Call Doctor Jamison," he said into the device. He heard it ring.

"G'day," a female voice said.

"Inna? That you?" he asked.

"That's right mate," she replied.

"You sound like a blooming Aussie. You sure it's you?"

"I saw your name on the tele window, so I thought I'd give you a real down-under welcome home. Bet you want to talk with my husband. Am I right?"

"Oh, I donno. You've made me smile. Just know that I'm ready for the holidays and spending them with me mum and da, you and the doc. Jus tell 'em all that I'm on my way. See you in a few hours."

-ୡ୭-

The flight was short. But it gave Noah more time to think about Gino and Kate and his own image. Why would any woman be interested in a tall Native American with an Aussie accent?

I don't fit into this skin.

Perhaps his fantasies about Kate were nothing more than that . . . fantasies. She could have anyone she wanted. Why would she want him, a student with no career? No, he felt certain she would never want to be anything more than his friend.

Gino may not be worthy, but neither am I.

At the same time he realized that if Kate knew of her boyfriend's infidelities, she would drop him like the garbage he was. Too bad Noah hadn't recorded the encounters on his cell phone. Telling Kate about what he had witnessed would be so much more difficult without that.

Chapter 38

Angry Words

Kate pushed the "end" button on her cell phone, willing away the words she had just read in a text.

I didn't want to have to tell you, but I caught your friend kissing another woman."

How could she have been so stupid? After that wonderful evening and the following days with Gino in Australia, she didn't want to believe Noah's words. Yet she heard the ring of truth in them. She ran through what she knew of Gino. Sure, he had been friendly with other women when she first met him, but no one had ever been so attentive, so loving as he had been these days. Over the course of their relationship, he had grown and he had even hinted at marriage. He had whispered over and over again that he loved her and wanted to spend the rest of his life with her. He had even given her a gold necklace with a teardrop diamond pendant as a token of his undying love.

Still, she couldn't imagine why Noah would say such nasty things if they weren't true. She felt as if her world were spiraling out of control. If she were to ask Gino about the accusation, she knew what he would say—that it was all a cheap, ugly lie. He would demand she unfriend Noah on her Facebook and remove his phone number from her cell phone, block all calls and texts from him.

To give herself time to think, she hummed. Sometimes humming helped her relax and lowered her stress level. But her humming grew raspy as the anger poured out in her voice.

She attempted to shift gears from her thoughts about Noah and his text, to the plans that she and Gino and their managers had arranged. Six weeks from now they would meet in Italy to sing a series of duets at the Teatro alla Scala in Milan, and while there they would celebrate her twenty-first birthday on Valentine's Day. How could they possibly make good music together with this cloud hanging over their heads?

It seemed that the world clamored for the two of them to be together, as though it were destined to be. Yet she didn't even know if she and Gino held the same religious beliefs. What *did* she really know about him, when it came right down to it? When she was Liz, she had been an agnostic, but she found God in the middle of her traumatic rebirth as Kate. She didn't know what Gino practiced because they had never discussed religion. She pulled out a pad of paper and made a list of things they should discuss. Religion was at the top of her list. Next came his feelings about fidelity . . . about *her*. Did he love her, or did he just think they made a good singing duo?

So many loose ends.

She thought back on her childhood as Kate and recalled the wonderful times that she had spent at her grandparent's home on Love Creek Road in Ben Lomond. It was the music that had first filled her spirit. It was a loving place where hymns were sung and instruments were played in worship. There had been a sense of calm and love all around. She missed those times.

Grandpa had been the strong stalwart of the family. It shocked them all when, two years ago, he suddenly passed away from a massive stroke. The big house wasn't the same after he was gone and now Grandma could no longer care for the property by herself. Kate had just learned that next week Grandma Kelly would be moving into her old bedroom at the Craig household in Castro Valley.

So many things were changing. Life was becoming complicated.

At least both Marcy and Bruce were sending her pictures and information about Mark, and she was keeping tabs on Megan via Facebook and text messages. Kate, Bruce, and Marcy all hoped that by attending college and living on campus, Megan would get over Josh.

However, Kate now knew that her cryptic attempts at ending the relationship had all but backfired. It seemed that Megan was more determined than ever to be with Josh. Perhaps, Kate thought, she should have taken the opposite stance and not only condoned the relationship, as she had in the beginning, but encouraged it. If Megan was at all like she had been at her age, pushing him on her might have caused her to dump him.

I can only pray for divine intervention.

CHAPTER 39

WEDDING DAY

Megan glanced down at her watch. Ten minutes late. She stood at the edge of campus, waiting for Josh who was running behind. She'd just been sent another email from Kate, giving reasons why Josh wasn't right for her. Everyone seemed to want to tell Megan what to do and how to live. Her parents kept telling her he was too old for her, and that she needed to put college and a career first. Why couldn't she have all three?

Impatiently, she huffed as she took in the strange weather. It wasn't so much that anything was out of the ordinary, really. It was a warm January day, nothing special. The sky was blue with few clouds, but everyone on campus seemed more subdued and an unnatural stillness had settled over the students. Normally, she might hear dogs barking or tires screeching, but today everything seemed hushed, as though the earth had taken a deep breath.

Or maybe she was just imagining things. Maybe she was just looking at the world through a different lens today because she and Josh had made a decision. They had decided to elope.

She knew her mom and dad would be angry, but she was tired of always having to explain their relationship. Besides, what was their problem with Josh?

She struggled with her backpack, wishing Josh would hurry. It was getting heavy. She watched as two girls passed, giggling with their heads together. Once upon a time, she had been like that, but it seemed so long ago now. That's what her parents didn't understand. She was growing up, becoming more responsible. When had she become so mature?

Her shoulders were beginning to hurt. Finally, she put the blue bag down to wait. Just as she did, she saw Josh's blue Ford round the corner and pull up next to her.

"What took you so long?" she asked, wondering if she was ready for this day. The dress in her backpack was probably all wrinkled by now. This wasn't how she had imagined her wedding day, alone at the courthouse, just her and Josh, but she was through fighting all the negativity. She was in love. Couldn't her family understand that? And Josh loved her too.

"Sorry, I've been working shifts and weekends to pay off my student loans. There was a last minute emergency . . . got here as fast as I could. Hop in!" he said, throwing the remainders of a food wrapper into the back seat.

As she went to enter the car, she swayed a little, nearly losing her balance.

"What was that?" she said. "It felt like the earth was moving."

"Probably just lightheaded. Did you eat lunch?"

She had to admit that she'd been so busy making preparations for her wedding day that she had forgotten to take time to eat.

"We'll pick you up something on the way," he said, taking her hand. "Are you ready?"

His eyes glistened. She still wasn't sure she was doing the right thing, but she was determined to go through with it.

"Let's do this!" she said.

"That's my girl," Josh said, revealing his pearly white teeth. After she'd buckled up, he pulled out into traffic.

Today was her wedding day, and nothing and no one could stop them.

Megan's heart skipped a beat. Here she was, on her way to becoming a wife and she hadn't even told Adriana. She was so excited at the prospect of eloping with her "true love" that at first she didn't even feel the car dance. Then it dawned on her.

"Stop Josh!" she yelled. The car swerved and hit a side-rail and came to a screeching halt. Another car rammed into theirs. "Oh my God, Josh, it's an earthquake. I'm scared. This is the biggest one I've ever felt."

Just then flames shot up from a distant building, and Megan could see that the street itself was cracked and sunken in places. Traffic was at a standstill.

Josh put his arms around her. "Are you hurt?"

"No, no. Just a little shook up," she answered.

Josh lifted her chin so that she was looking straight at him. "We can't stay here. We need to find a way to get onto another side street that's undamaged."

"Josh, my family, your family. They may be hurt. We can't go on with our plans. We have to go back and help."

"I know," he said. "Where do you want to start?"

"Can you get us to the high school? I know it well since I went there last year. We're only four miles from it. I want to see if Mark is okay. Can you do it?"

"I'll do the best I can," he said as he put the car into reverse. As he did so, a hubcap fell off. He ignored it and inched his way, partially on the cracked sidewalk, to the next street corner and turned right.

It took an hour to travel the four miles, but when Megan saw the school with the windows broken out and hundreds of kids in disarray on the lawn, she was shocked at the extent of the injuries and damage.

Some students were bleeding and crying while others were acting like it had been a thrill ride. Some were tending the needs of others and some were comforting the traumatized. It was a surreal picture of humanity and how differently humans deal with disaster.

Both Josh and Megan jumped out of the car. Josh popped open the trunk and grabbed a first-aid kit. "I always carry one for my shifts as an EMT."

It was how he put himself through college. Although Megan had known what he did on weekends and two evenings a week, until that moment, she hadn't realized how strong and capable he was. Now she saw him differently. He was mature and almost business-like. He fit well into her family profile—maybe too well. Her father was an X-ray tech at Kaiser, and her stepmother was a physical therapist at Stanford. She tried to process this while assessing the chaotic scene. She ran across the lawn calling out for Mark.

As she and Josh moved through the throng of students, Josh stopped twice to tend injured kids. He applied pressure, gauze, and tight tape to stop their bleeding and assured each one that they would be alright. Megan did whatever Josh said: "Help me hold his arm; Get more tape out of the kit; Go back to the car and get the bottled water."

As she ran zigzagging past students to get to the car, she heard a familiar voice. "Megan. Over here!" It came from the far left. It was Mark. He was holding his leg, and sweat was pouring down his face. He was soaked from head to toe. "I'm hurt. Help me, please."

"Hold on," Megan yelled. "I'll get Josh."

"He's here too? And what are you doing here?" Mark asked, his face screwed up from the pain.

"Don't ask," Megan replied. "Just consider yourself lucky. Josh is a trained EMT."

"A what?" Mark said.

"An emergency medical technician. Right now he's helping another student. I'll go get him."

As soon as she found Josh, he rushed to finish what he was doing and then ran over to study Mark's injured leg.

"How did this happen?" he asked.

"It was during break between classes. I was in the bathroom when it hit. I tried to get under one of the sinks for protection, but the darn thing broke loose and fell on my leg. Water was squirting everywhere. I'm just lucky that my head wasn't in the same spot that my leg was, or I'd have been a goner."

"Your leg is broken," Josh said. "I'll need to make a splint. Megan, see if you can find a three-foot length of wood or something similar. A flat piece of wood—two if you can find 'em. I need to mobilize his leg above the knee and down past the ankle. I also need some clothing or something soft for padding. I have tape."

Megan wasn't about to go into the school. Aftershocks were still causing plaster to fall and glass was everywhere. She rushed to the baseball field and searched the bleachers, which were damaged too. Fortunately, she was able to pull some loose boards from the front of the dugout. It was the best she could do. She ran back, dropped the wooden slats next to Josh, then removed her heavy sweater for the needed padding.

"What's next?" she asked.

"You were going to get water from the car. We still need it."

Megan ran across the campus. When she reached the car another aftershock hit. She held onto the door handle and lowered herself to the sidewalk. She felt as though the world was coming to an end. She started crying and praying at the same time. "Please, I don't want to die." She heard something crashing and distant sirens mingled with screams and moans.

The rumbling stopped. She felt her face. With both hands she wiped the tears away. Then, she didn't know why, but she got angry. She jumped upright, yanked open the car door and grabbed the two bottles of water. A surge of energy rushed through her as she ran back to Josh and Mark's side.

She opened one of the bottles of water, gave it to Mark and then turned to Josh and said, "I think we should abandon the car and carry Mark back to the house. It's only about eight blocks. It will be faster than driving. The traffic is at a standstill. Besides I'm worried about my parents and Shaun. I want to see if the house is still standing and look for Shaun."

"Okay," Josh said. "Quick give your mom and dad a call, make sure they're okay, then I'll contact mine too."

For the next few minutes they tried one phone after another, to no avail. Frustrated, she and Josh eyed Mark.

"You're bigger than I remember," Josh said, "but Megan and I will each take a side. You may have to hop on one leg while we hold you up."

With that settled, they began the long trek home.

Noah was enjoying the warm, less sultry weather after his stay in Australia. He had only been back for a week and already it felt much longer, he realized as he made his way across campus. Kate had texted him apology after apology for days after her friend's rude behavior. And although he had assured her he understood, she had followed up with an ecard saying **"I'm sorry."** The picture on the front of the ecard was of a koala hugging a teddy bear with a giant heart on its tummy.

He'd spoken to his mum about what he'd witnessed between Kate's friend and the other girls, and she had assured him she was doing the right thing by telling Kate. But she'd also warned him that she might not welcome the bad tidings, and to expect that she might not take it well.

Although he had prepared himself for the possibility, it had nonetheless come as a deep wound when she hadn't responded after he had sent the text, telling of the singer's infidelity. Each day that passed convinced him that it might have been the right thing morally, to tell her, but it had come at a huge cost. He ran his fingers through his hair, wondering at the stillness of the day. It was as though the silence of his cell phone, now that he no longer received her daily pings, had reflected itself in the weather. Odd.

He had two minutes to finish his cross campus trek or he'd be late to his next class when he felt a sudden jerk. It wasn't enough to cause him to lose his balance—more like someone had run into something nearby. Although Australia had earthquakes from time to time, Melbourne was not an area that was affected by them, so this was an unknown factor to him. But he noticed that the top of the flagpole was swinging back and forth.

"Did you feel that?" asked a fellow student, who was on his bicycle and had come to a stop next to Noah. He stood for a second, legs straddling the bike. "Bet that was a big one on the San Andreas Fault."

"A big one?" Noah said.

"Yeah, an earthquake. They don't originate here, but when a big one hits the Bay Area, we feel the rumble . . . always some damage here, but not major."

The young man took out his cell phone and listened to a news station. "Wow! They say it was a 7.6. That's really bad."

Noah's thoughts went to those at Stanford Hospital. Were they okay? So many wonderful people who had cared for him might be hurt.

Kate had just finished changing after her Friday night performance when her manager, Cassie, barged through the dressing room door. "There's been a major earthquake in the Bay Area. It's a big one. I tried to get through to my family, but all the lines are busy. I couldn't get anything. Oh, Kate, I know your family is there too. I don't know what to do."

Kate flew to her cell phone and texted a message to her mother.

No response.

She texted Josh, believing that he was still at the University of Oregon.

Did u hear about earthquake in CA? I can't get hold of Mom. U try.

She read his response.

I'm in CA. Will call & try to get home.

Chapter 40

Life and Death

Kate sat with Josh and her parents in the front row of the chapel as the pastor recounted the life of Katherine Kelly, Kate's grandmother and namesake. As she fingered the hymnal, she felt a great emptiness, the same emptiness she had felt when she'd received the news that her grandmother had a fatal heart attack during the earthquake; the stress had been too much for her. It seemed like every time she turned around she was losing someone she loved. Once again, so much had changed.

If Grandma had stayed in Ben Lomond, if she'd never moved into my bedroom, would she still be alive?

Thank goodness for Kate's mother, who dabbed at her eyes with one hand while clutching Kate's hand tightly with the other.

Gino had been on tour still and hadn't been able to get away. She tried to convince herself that it didn't hurt, but it still stung anyway. Surely, he could have come if he'd really wanted to, but then she reminded herself how hard it was to cancel a show and all the people who would be affected if he rushed to her side. She squeezed her mother's hand tighter, happy to have her at her side as they listened to the rest of the sermon.

When the pastor completed his remarks and a prayer, he called upon Kate and Josh to sing. Kate knew that this duet would be the most difficult one she had ever performed in public. She wasn't sure if she could hold back the tears. Determined not to cry, she squared her shoulders, looked up toward heaven, and mouthed the words, "This is for you, Grandma."

Josh walked up to the microphone and said, "Our mother told us that our grandma was singing this song when she died. Please sing *Amazing Grace* with us."

As they had done so many years ago at family gatherings in their grandparents' Ben Lomond home, she and her brother sang in two-part harmony. The congregation joined in.

Kate lifted her voice in tribute to the loving memory of the woman who had given her the family pendant and who had brought her, through love and music, into a close relationship with God.

As she sang, she thought of Gino, how he had chosen career over her and her needs. Then and there she made a promise to herself that her career would never interfere with her values, her beliefs, and her vow to serve others. She had so much to live for, and she feared that she had become as callused and selfish in her rise to fame as Gino. It had taken a death to realize that.

After the service, friends gathered in the dining hall for refreshments and to share stories about Katherine Kelly. Kate told stories about picking blackberries on her grandparents' property and Grandma using them to bake pies. She also told stories about the dog, Corky, that her grandparents raised. He always smiled when guests arrived, though many thought he was baring his teeth in threat. But Grandma always told them to watch his wagging tail—it demonstrated his joy. He was just saying "welcome" in his own way by smiling as best he could.

When the guests left, Kate and her family gathered the flower arrangements that had been delivered. So many friends and family members had sent beautiful floral tributes.

"You need to read this card, Kate," her mother said.

Kate looked at the card that accompanied the large wreath of yellow roses. It read,

Dearest Kate and family, I can only offer my heartfelt condolences. Thinking of you and praying for you, just as you once did for me. Yours truly, Noah Burnett.

Gino had forgotten to send even flowers for the funeral, much less a heartfelt card. Kate's hand went to her pendant, an automatic reaction whenever she felt overwhelmed. How could she have treated him so unfairly? She had never contacted him back after he'd texted her about Gino. She had been so humiliated and felt so foolish. Even he could see what she hadn't: Her desperate need to feel love had blinded her; Gino could never be a true love for her. She wanted to believe that a leopard could change its spots, but she wasn't so sure anymore. As her grandmother liked to say "the proof is in the pudding, darlin'." Kate just hoped she hadn't burned a bridge with Noah. He had been a good friend. Maybe he could be even more, if she let him . . .

The next day, Kate sent a friend request on her "friends and family" Facebook account to Noah. She mailed a handwritten thank you note and an apology and asked him to call her. She wondered whether she was forgiving him or herself . . . maybe both.

CHAPTER 41

VALENTINE'S DAY

The flight from Melbourne to New Zealand would take a few hours, time that Jamison needed to figure out what to do with the rest of his life. He didn't know why his thoughts were in such disarray. This trip was supposed to be a Valentine's gift from him to the love of his life, Inna.

Inna sat quietly next to him reading one of her many novels and sipping a cola. She was dressed in a light gray pantsuit with a strain of simple pearls at her neck. It seemed to Jamison that Inna was always happy. She was outgoing and formed new friendships wherever she went.

It was her talent, but not his. Jamison didn't have her friendly habit of reaching out to others. He wasn't sure whether it was innate shyness or his inability to chat about such mundane things as the weather. All he felt sure of now was that Noah seemed comfortable in his studies and any earlier fears of organ rejection were small. Therefore, his efforts to help Noah were all but concluded.

He felt depressed. It had been such a high for him to be back in the thick of the world of medicine, and saving Noah's life had been a thrill. He wondered if reliving those wonderful days would be enough to last the months and years ahead.

I don't want to shut myself in again. But of what use am I now?

"You okay?" Inna asked. "You look so pensive."

"No. I'm fine. We should have a good time this week at the timeshare. It's highly rated and there are lots of activities nearby."

"Then why are you rubbing your knuckles? You do that when you're troubled by something. I know you too well."

"No. It's just a little arthritis. Just trying to warm them up."

Inna shook her head. "I don't buy that. You've never complained about arthritis. What's bugging you?"

Jamison hung his head and whispered, "I don't feel relevant. It's that simple." He lifted his head and looked at her. "Now that Noah is well and others are getting the gift of a second life, my work is done."

"That's silly, Donald. Now is the time to celebrate your achievements. What more can you ask for than to be responsible for a breakthrough procedure that could save hundreds, if not thousands, of lives?"

Jamison took in a deep breath. "You don't understand. I was on top of the world when Noah awoke from his surgery. I was ecstatic when he walked out of the hospital on his own. But that was then. This is now. I feel as though my life's work is over. Do I just sit back and gloat over yesterday?"

Inna took his hand and held it for the duration of the flight.

Jamison stood waiting for Inna's and his luggage to come down the shoot. Even after the six-hour flight, his trousers still held a firm crease and his shirt looked newly pressed. Although he had fidgeted with his hands most of the way to Australia, he had otherwise sat stone upright with only his mind and hands in gear. *So much tension.*

As luggage began entering the turnstile, a fellow passenger distracted him. "Aren't you the doctor in the newspaper?" the man asked loudly. "You are! I recognize you from the newspaper."

Others who were standing nearby started pointing at him and then Jamison overheard his name being mentioned. He turned to the stranger and said, "Yes, I'm Donald Jamison." The man motioned to a woman standing a few feet away. "Margaret, come over here. This is the doctor who developed the brain-transplant surgery."

The woman stumbled over and touched his sleeve. "Doctor Jamison, I can't believe it's you. It's a miracle. We need your help. Our daughter—you need to help our daughter," she said.

Jamison looked over at Inna, who smiled as if to say, *See? You will always have value.*

Today was a special day—not just Valentine's Day, but Adriana's birthday and, as Marcy knew, Kate's birthday too. Ten years ago, when she was introduced to Kate's surgical case, the first thing that she had noted on the chart was that her daughter, Adriana, and her patient were born on the same day just two years apart.

Despite the horrors of the January earthquake, life did go on. Marcy tried to look forward to the dinner date that Bruce had planned for tonight, yet she couldn't help but think back to that day and the enormous losses that it caused. Tragically, two hundred and eight lives were lost and more than 3,500 were injured. There had been some damage to the bridges, but they were basically intact. Although the governor had declared a state of emergency and federal aid had poured in, it would be weeks, maybe months, before things would be back to normal. Several streets had been repaired, but miles of cracked and sunken roadway still remained impassable; temporary modular classrooms had been set up at Mark's high school while it was being rebuilt; Shaun's school was back in full swing since it had been retrofitted the year before and it now met the highest earthquake standards.

Marcy had been part of the staff who helped assess the losses and damages at Stanford Hospital. Two patients had died during the quake: one man during an emergency surgery, and an elderly woman who had been in critical condition before the quake struck. Neither left the hospital liable.

Supplies were destroyed, rooms needed repair, and patients had to be moved. On the other hand, the Hayward Kaiser facility where Bruce worked had minor damage, but repairs were quickly made. *So life continues.*

Marcy rubbed her aching shoulder and sat on the edge of the bed. Closer to home, she had been so proud of Megan and Josh for their quick action. Despite that, she still felt uneasy about their relationship. Although the trauma of the quake had drawn on both of their resources and they had performed wonderfully together to help the students, it was also a reality check. They both needed to finish school and get settled in careers before they married.

Megan told her that by the time she and the boys had arrived at the house, Shaun had already found his way home.

"I got scared," he told Marcy and Bruce when they were finally all together. "Some of the girls were crying, and even some of the boys, so I left the schoolyard and walked home." Then, as if to ease their fears, he added, "But it was no big deal."

Apparently Josh had carried Mark in, cleaned him up, set his leg, and had given him some pain relievers. Then, as a precaution, Megan had turned off the gas and checked the house for damage.

Marcy hadn't returned home until the next day. She stayed to help the panicked patients and the incoming injured. Plus, damages to the roads and backed-up traffic would have made leaving nearly impossible. She had learned that her kids were okay via cell phone, clinching her decision to stay.

Adriana had called and let everyone know that she was alright, too. There had been some damage on the campus and classes were cancelled, but transportation wasn't up and running so she couldn't come home for the week.

It took Bruce two days to get home, but on his way, he drove to San Jose State and picked up Adriana so, for a brief period, the family had been together.

Now it was Valentine's Day. Despite the turmoil, Marcy was joyful that Bruce not only remembered that today was a day for romance and flowers, but had made reservations at one of the chic boutique restaurants nearby that had somehow survived the quake without a scratch. It wasn't extravagant, but they had much to celebrate. Their children and home had survived. Mark was the only one injured and he was on the mend. Some fine China, a few framed wall pictures, and a lamp or two needed replacement, but the family had been lucky.

Marcy got up from the bed and began dressing for the evening. As she put on her classiest pants suit, she wondered at the timing of the quake and how it had interrupted Josh and Megan's impulsive elopement plans. *Providence. Fate.* She hoped that there would be a cooling off period.

Megan sat cross-legged on the grassy commons at her university, unconsciously plucking individual strands of grass as she dialed her mother's number. She'd had a lot of time to think since the earthquake. Had she been rushing into things with Josh just to show her family that she could be independent? Maybe.

And did she want to end up like her mom, having a baby early and juggling all the needs of a home, a husband, work, and a family? She wasn't sure she was ready for that. Some women never got back on track once they let their hopes and dreams fall to the wayside. She hated to admit that her parents might be right. Besides, if Josh really loved her, he would wait until she was ready for all of that.

The cell phone rang twice before her mother answered.

"Hi, Megan. Happy Valentine's Day. What's up?" Marcy said.

"Mom, Josh and I have been talking." Megan paused, giving herself time to form the right words. "I just don't want to make the same mistakes that my mother made—you know, getting married too soon, starting a family. But I truly love him. I do."

It was Marcy's turn to pause. Finally, she said, "Life is complicated, but you're a smart young woman and Josh is an intelligent man. You have plenty of time to finish your education and he needs to find work in his chosen field. Then you two can take on the responsibilities and challenges of marriage and a family."

Megan felt a wave of relief. "That's what we think too. We decided that we'll see each other when our schedules permit. But for now, we'll take it easy." There, she'd said it.

"I'm proud of you two," Marcy said. "Smart decision. I love you lots."

"I love you too," Megan said. "Happy Valentine's Day, Mom."

"You too. I hope that you are helping Adriana celebrate her birthday today. Tell her to give me a call. I want to see if she got the gift that we sent."

Megan was about to hang up when Marcy said, "Do you mind if I text your dad and tell him what you said about taking it easy with Josh?"

"No, go for it."

"Okay, hold on and let's see what he says."

Megan could hear her mom typing the text as she waited, her hand unconsciously bunching the grass at her side. Finally, her mother came back on the line.

"Wanna hear what he had to say?" she asked.

"Go for it," Megan said, curious how he would respond.

"He wrote back, 'Whew.'"

Marcy laughed along with Megan. How like her dad to make it simple and to the point. Maybe they were all feeling the same thing. *Whew.*

Kate smiled at her image in the mirror, not because she was pleased with her appearance, but because she was recalling how fantastic the last few days had been. After her epiphany with Noah, she had confronted Gino and made it clear that she would no longer accept his cheating ways. Either he was with her or he wasn't, he couldn't have it both ways. She had made a list of what she expected in a relationship. To her surprise, he had agreed to everything on her list. He had promised to change his ways. He had even offered to convert.

Even more surprising, she and Gino had discussed marriage. Soon they would plan their family and make America their home base. And best of all, today was her twenty-first birthday . . . everything she had ever dreamed of was coming true . . . like a fairytale. Now she just hoped he would keep his end of the bargain.

She sang as she zipped up her fuchsia silk dress and buckled her fuchsia and gold-studded Grecian-style shoes. She donned her heavy black stole and grabbed her purse and a gift-wrapped package. She had ordered him a beautiful hand-knitted scarf and written a love song, which she planned to sing to him. Then she placed her gifts in a white box and carefully wrapped them in shiny silver paper. She had finished it off with a large blue ribbon.

She didn't care that it was cold and raining outside, because she felt a warm glow. She was as excited as a schoolgirl. Yet her thirty-nine-year-old brain pondered which half of her was running the show—her brain or her heart: the wisdom that comes with the aging of one's gray matter or her young body's hormones. No time to think about that now. She hurried toward the door and down the hotel hallway, eager to put such thoughts behind her.

Tonight would be her turn to surprise Gino. The evening plans were to start at seven o'clock and it was only six.

Kate and Gino were on separate floors at the hotel. She couldn't stop beaming as she entered the elevator and pushed the down button to the fourth floor. When she arrived at his door, she removed her cloak and draped it over her arm. She wanted to look spectacular. She knocked twice and waited. No answer. She knocked again and wondered if perhaps he was in the shower. Maybe surprising him wasn't such a good idea.

"Who is it?" he asked through the closed door.

"It's me, Kate. Open up. I have something for you."

"You're early, I said seven."

"I know. Remember the time you came to my door early? I sent you away, but not tonight. Open the door. I have a gift for you."

She heard another voice in the room . . . a woman's voice.

"Who's with you?" she asked.

"No one. It's the TV."

"Open the door, Gino."

The door opened slightly and Gino peered through the crack. "Come back later. I'm not dressed," he said.

Kate looked at the face of the man to whom she had promised herself and saw a smear of bright red lipstick on his mouth. She thought of Bruce's warning and Noah's text telling her of Gino's infidelity. She felt like such a fool.

At that moment, something snapped in her. She shoved the door wide and spotted one of the young hotel maids hiding behind the door, her back against the wall. Then she doubled up her fist, reared back and swung forward with all her one hundred pounds aimed for his nose. She hit him as hard as she could. He reeled backward holding his bleeding nose as Kate glared at the pair. The young woman hunched her shoulders into a "so what" motion and giggled.

Kate tore open the gift she had brought and pulled the song she'd written out first, stuffing it in her pocket. Then she reached in and grabbed the hand-knitted scarf, wrapped it around her neck, and marched out of the room.

Gino called out, "Kate! Don't go. I'm sorry!"

Kate never looked back. From now on she would only look forward, to her future. And she had a strong feeling that that future might just be with Noah. She would never know until she gave him a call, which she planned to do now.

Valentine's Day was more than a day for romance according to Noah; it was also a time to show family and close friends his affection. He had already sent email cards to his Aussie family and to Donald and Inna Jamison. *And a special one to Kate.*

But today he was spending hours making a card for his Whitehorse family to thank them for their sacrifice and caring. He used colored paper, flowers and glue, then cut out images of hearts and some glitter that ended up on his face and under his nails. His large hands made him feel clumsy, so he took great care with every cut and paste job. But his love was best transcribed by the words he typed:

My dearest Diana, Aileen, and Earl—my Whitehorse Family, Love is akin to grace. Thank you for your love. Thank you for your grace. Although I can never take the place of Kevin, I can love you all so completely that, hopefully, it will provide some small measure of comfort for your loss. You and Kevin were there for me and I pledge that I will always be there for you.

All my respect and love, Noah.

He printed his words on paper, cut them to fit on a space he had provided on the huge card, and pasted them on.

Before he left his room to deliver his gift, he checked his email. He saw that there was something from Kate. He clicked to open it. His heart beat faster as he read the Valentine. Her words were sweet, maybe even a touch romantic. He smiled, recognizing the foot in the door. He hoped.

Every day, Kate was in his thoughts. He watched all the YouTube videos and followed her performances. Those weeks when she had shut him out were the loneliest and most depressing since the operation. Maybe they would only remain good friends.

If that's all she will give me, then I'll gladly take it.

Of course he had sent her an ecard too. But he'd been careful to make it a friend-to-friend note. He never wanted to anger her again or to lose touch with her. She was like a beacon of hope, an example of a life well lived. Despite their earlier mishap, he admired her above all others.

He tucked in his shirt, picked up the card and a grocery bag from his desk, and walked briskly into the living room.

He was the first one home that day, but he knew that all three would be home within the hour. He placed the card in the middle of the dining room table. Then he went to the refrigerator and brought out a carved pineapple filled with fresh fruit. Next, he took out a three-tiered serving tray and arranged the store-bought cookies and truffles. Finally, he took two floral placemats from the bureau and placed them on either side of the card, then put the pineapple and food tray on them. Then he stood back to evaluate his handiwork. It wasn't perfect, but he thought it would convey his respect and devotion to his second family.

Life was good.

Chapter 42

An Invitation

For weeks now, Kate and Noah had been corresponding, even talking late into the night by phone. Kate knew more about him than she'd ever known about any other man, and she realized that she liked what she knew of him. He was kind, thoughtful, and possibly *the* most caring man she'd ever known. His texts and emails were ones she would read over several times and would savor his words.

It was still very early, but she scanned her emails in hopes that she would find another tidbit. Nothing yet from Noah, but she saw one from Marcy with the subject line: *Invitation to a picnic.* She clicked to open it:

We understand that you are finishing up your performances in New York this week and hoped you would honor us with your presence at a family picnic. On Saturday, June 23, 11:00 a.m., please meet us at Lake Elizabeth in Fremont at the paddleboat rental booth. Just bring yourself. We will have refreshments, and there are concession stands if we need to supplement the food and drink in our baskets. Both Megan and Adriana are home for the break so all four of our kids will be there. They may bring friends. We will rent paddleboats for an outing if the weather remains as lovely as it is today. Dogs are permitted, so we will bring Algae. Your brother, Josh, was invited too, but says he can't make it—has other plans. Let us know if you can make it.

Yours truly,

Marcy Lindsay

Kate grabbed her cell phone and punched the contact number for her manager, Cassie.

"Hi, Kate. What is it?"

"Cassie, please make me flight reservations into Oakland for next Tuesday. I need to visit with my family and have plans to meet the Lindsay family for an outing," Kate said.

"Isn't that the family that you invited to the San Francisco gala a couple of years ago?" she asked.

"Yes. And I'm so excited. I need a little rest time with my mom and dad, and time to catch up with my friends."

"Consider it done," Cassie said.

"Thanks. I owe you one."

"No. You owe me two . . . or maybe just a raise or a giant bonus," Cassie said with a laugh.

"Consider it done," Kate said.

She grinned from ear to ear as she called Marcy's cell phone. It rang six times before the voicemail came on. "Hi, Marcy. It's Kate. This is my most positive RSVP. Thanks, girlfriend. Can't wait to see all of you."

Kate put down the cell phone and danced around the hotel room. Next week would be the first time in ten plus years since she had last laid eyes on her son. Marcy and Bruce had messaged her pictures of him at his graduation two weeks ago. He was only seven years old the last time she had kissed him. It had only been a peck on the cheek as she had rushed out the door. She wondered whether he would pull away from her if she tried to touch him.

Does he have a girlfriend? Is he smart like his dad? So many questions raced through her head. *Ten years . . . ten long years.*

Bruce had kept his promise. It had taken a while, but he had been good for his word.

Chapter 43

Picnic in the Park

Kate arrived a good fifteen minutes early so she could refamiliarize herself with the layout. Many years ago, she and Bruce had picnicked at this very park when the kids were just toddlers.

She took in the sights and sounds, but most of all she took in the smells. Plants were in bloom, the water had a fresh smell of its own, and the grass was green from the springtime rains. The mature trees provided shade and some displayed their floral wares. A flock of egret bathed and dined near a rocky bank, and Canadian geese and ducks abounded. She watched where she stepped as she crossed the lawns to get a closer look at the expanse of the lake. Boaters were already out enjoying the perfect weather.

She stopped at one of the concession stands and purchased a cold drink. Then she sat at a small table by herself and tried to picture what today would be like. She hoped that there would be a moment or two when she could touch Mark, maybe ruffle his hair or tease him and get a reaction—anything to create a connection between them.

When the appointed hour grew near, she tossed the plastic bottle in a recycle container and walked over to the paddleboat dock. Bruce, Marcy, and the family were already there. Kate half-skipped and threw her arms around Marcy.

"Thank you both for inviting me to your outing. I really needed a break," she said. Kate reached for Megan, but the family dog, Algae, leaped up and planted a sloppy tongue on Kate's chin, almost knocking her over. His tail was wagging faster than an automatic windshield wiper in a downpour.

"Down boy," Megan yelled. Then she looked at Kate with wrinkled brow and tilted her head as though trying to remember something. "I'm so sorry. Algae never does this to strangers. He's always so docile around people that he doesn't know." Then she looked up as though trying to recall something. "Well, there was another time . . . oh never mind, forget it."

"It's okay. I love animals, and Algae looks like a frisky fellow," she said as she scratched Algae under the chin. Kate smiled to herself. Algae saw her, *knew* her, just as he had several years ago when she had tried to steal a glimpse of her former family.

For a moment, Kate thought about throwing herself onto the lawn and wrestling with old Algae like she had in years gone by. But she resisted the urge.

"Kate," Bruce said. "I want you to meet our sons, Mark and Shaun. They've heard a lot about you. They know that Marcy was your physical therapist."

Kate reached her hand out first to Shaun and shook his hand. "So happy to make your acquaintance," she said.

Shaun smiled back sheepishly. "Yeah, me too."

Then she reached over to Mark. An emotional wave hit her that was more powerful than Algae recognizing her. He was so tall, so handsome—like a young Bruce. But she could see hints of Liz in his smile. She felt her chin start to quiver and a lump form in her throat. To hide this, she cleared her throat and said, "I would have recognized you as Bruce's son right off." She took his hand and could swear she felt his soul. Although she had seen his pictures, the flesh and blood Mark was so much more than she had dreamed. Her baby boy was a man.

"Hi, Kate," he said. Then he pulled a young woman forward. "This here's my girlfriend, Chloe."

Kate let go of her son's hand and looked at the teenage girl who was staring all moon-faced at Mark. Chloe had strawberry blonde hair and freckles across her nose. She was about the same height that Liz had been. Kate acknowledged the girl and said something friendly to her. Then she glanced over at Bruce and they exchanged a knowing grin. Mark, like Algae, hadn't forgotten Liz. His choice of a girlfriend was as close to the image of his birth mother as one could be, not counting the tattoo of a kitten on the girl's ankle.

"What about us?" Megan said as she and Adriana moved to her side.

Kate hugged them both and for a moment held her daughter's soft hand. It was a happy day, a perfect day. The sun seemed to bless the hours that Kate and the Lindsay family shared.

Toward the late afternoon, ominous clouds blew in and a sudden clap of thunder followed by a downpour ended the outing. But it didn't diminish the joy Kate felt.

CHAPTER 44

A NEW DAY

Kate looked out upon the hundreds of music lovers that sat on lawn chairs or blankets spread out across the lawns. She was back—another opera in the park, another opening of the San Francisco opera season. And a chance to see her family . . . *and Noah.*

She massaged her arm, practiced breathing exercises, and smiled at all that had transpired in such a short span of time. It had been four years since the last time she had sung here. So much had changed. But she was content. Her relationship with Marcy and Bruce was friendly and she received updates on all four kids. Megan and Josh were still in touch and, when their respective schedules permitted, they were still "seeing" each other.

Her manager, Cassie, had married and left the business two months ago, and last month announced that she was going to be a mother. Her new manager, Emily, was busy rearranging Kate's unruly locks.

"It's okay, Emily. Everything is going to be just fine. Let me peek around the portico. I have friends and a beau who said that they'd be here. I want to see if I can find them in the crowd."

"Okay. But it's just ten minutes until the program starts. Keep warming up."

Kate hummed as she poked her head around the structure and glanced at the hundreds of people, searching for her family.

There they were. Marcy, Bruce, and Shaun. Their blanket was almost in the same place that Marcy had placed it those four years ago. *Poor Shaun.* She knew that Marcy and Bruce had probably dragged him here kicking and complaining. Opera wasn't his thing, according to Bruce. But Megan, Adriana, and Mark weren't there. All three were back at college and unable to attend. Kate was warmed by the fact that Megan and Adriana had kept in touch and had sent their best wishes for today.

As Kate was about to turn around, she saw a tall dark-haired man wave at her. *Noah.* She waved back at her number one fan and Facebook buddy . . . *and she hoped something more.* He had said he would be there and asked if he could take her out after the event. She had quickly responded, "Yes."

She felt butterflies in her stomach. He looked like a Roman athlete statue except for the blue jeans and stylish jacket over a white shirt.

She felt a wide smile form, and she almost laughed out loud. This was a special day. She knew that he was still deep into his studies, but today was Sunday, and he had driven all the way from Sacramento to see her. She stood as straight as her five-foot-two body could stretch, squared her shoulders, and prepared for the many arias she would be singing. She wanted to make sure that Marcy, Bruce, Shaun, and especially Noah wouldn't be disappointed.

As music filled the stage and grounds, Kate entered the stage. The applause and shouts of adoration were welcoming. It hit a crescendo, then the applause fell silent as she began to sing the perilous "Per Pieta, Ben Mio" Fiordiligi's aria from Mozart's *Cosi Fan Tutte.* Her voice soared. She hit every note perfectly. It was a great beginning, and the rest of the afternoon was a success.

When the program came to a close, the audience broke out into shouts of "brava." For a single day, at least, she felt like she was home.

As the crowd thinned, Bruce and Marcy approached, dragging ten-year-old Shaun with them. Kate and Marcy hugged. Bruce nodded to Kate. "That was wonderful," he said.

"Yeah, you were real good," Shaun said. "I don't like opera, but you made me almost like it."

Kate laughed, but turned to greet Noah as he walked toward them. "Bruce, Marcy, Shaun, I want you to meet my good friend, Noah. The world's second brain-transplant survivor."

The trio gawked, then greeted the tall stranger. Kate watched as the conversation became animated. Marcy touched Noah's scar and commented on his robustness.

"I read about your story. It's amazing. And to think it was the same Dr. Jamison who acted as your mentor through it all," Marcy said.

"No ma'am, you're wrong. Dr. Jamison was the conduit for the surgery, but Miss Kate here was my mentor. She was there when I went in for the surgery and was there when I came out. She gave me the confidence that I would survive." He reached over and took Kate's hand. "She's my hero."

Kate felt her chest swell and she liked the warmth of his big hand on hers. She felt especially petite next to him. "I think it's time for a celebration," Kate said. "I know a wonderful place for fish and chips or crab claws down on the embarcadero. Would you mind?" she asked Noah. "We'll still have the rest of the evening afterward."

He shook his head and said, "That would be fine. We'll have plenty of time," he added with a mischievous smile.

"How about you, Shaun? You like fish and chips?"

"Yeah. Dad fixes me fish sticks all the time," Shaun replied.

Bruce ruffled Shaun's hair. "You'll like San Francisco's fish and chips even better," he said.

"Give me a minute or so while I go backstage and change into something more appropriate for the harbor. I'll be fast."

"I have my car here," Noah said, "so I can drive you—if you don't mind riding in a fifteen-year-old Blazer."

Kate glanced at Bruce and watched as he cringed. Bruce had owned a Blazer those twelve years ago when she, as Liz, was in that fatal accident in her Honda. The memory was bittersweet. Kate smiled sadly, then turned to Noah. "If you're a good driver, I'll be fine with that."

As Bruce and Noah made plans for where to meet, Kate dashed into the backstage area. "Emily," she shouted. Then she saw her manager picking up photos. "Thank god you're still here. Please take my gown back to the hotel. I'm going out with friends for dinner this evening."

"No problem. Bring me back something. I'm starving," said Emily.

"I will. I promise," Kate said as she rushed out to meet up with Noah.

When the fish and chips had been devoured, the five of them took a walk on Pier 39. Music played, vendors hawked their wares, acrobats performed, and even Shaun had to admit he was glad he had come. It was a grand evening, but as dusk dropped its opaque curtain, Bruce and Marcy agreed that it was time to head for home—school and work tomorrow. Kate and Noah said their goodbyes to the Lindsays, and Kate made a promise to call and set up special box seats for them on opening night.

"Shaun, do you want to come to the opera with your parents?" Kate asked.

"Nah, it's okay. I might need to study or somethin'," he said.

They all laughed at his attempt to bow out gracefully.

As the Lindsays left, Noah took Kate's hand. "It's time for me to take you home too." He walked her to the old Blazer and opened the door for her. "Where are you staying?" he asked.

"I'm at the Omni," she replied.

"Ah, yes, nothing but the best for the songbird of San Francisco. That's just a mile or so up the street, isn't it? Not much time to have a little more one-on-one conversation with my best girl."

Kate blushed as she realized that Noah was making a pass. She had hoped he would, but was cautious about her expectations after the fiasco with Gino.

He began to sing in a raspy Australian accent. "I'll take you home again Kathleen . . . er Katherine."

By the time he finished his attempt at serenade, they were at the hotel.

"Come up for a cup of tea?" Kate asked.

In answer, Noah jumped out of the car, opened the door for Kate and gave his keys to the valet. "I might be a little while," he said to the valet.

Kate took his hand as he helped her from the car. She finally felt ready for a relationship.

Chapter 45

Jamison's Reward

Jamison had never been in a parade before. He had known celebrity, but this was totally different. He sat in the back of the blue classic convertible with his wife at his side and waved at the crowd of admirers. He had once thought that getting the Nobel Prize was the pinnacle of success, but it was nothing compared to the love that his fellow Melbournians showered upon him.

The worldwide media heralded the many successful transplants and mentioned Jamison as the surgeon who had first performed the operation. And when Noah, an Aussie, became the second brain-transplant survivor, the nation suddenly became aware that this famous doctor was one of them.

Inna glanced over at him. "I think you are as popular as the prime minister."

"Heaven help me," he replied.

"Donald, these people really love you."

He chuckled as he raised his hand and continued waving. He had found a home. He was now "Physician Laureate" of the Melbourne Medical School and received the Order of Australia (AO) in the General Division of the Queen's Birthday Honours List.

"You know the best part of all this?" he said to Inna.

"No, tell me."

"I no longer sit at home each evening watching the telly. We have so many friends and organizations to attend. We are busy all the time. But, best of all, the last time I tried to form your face in clay, it came out looking like you . . . sort of."

Inna laughed and squeezed his non-waving hand. "Now you know why they call Melbourne the most livable city in the world."

Jamison grinned. "It has captured our hearts."

"And you've captured theirs."

Chapter 46

Unwelcomed News

Noah heard a knock on the hotel door and a voice from the other side saying, "Room service."

Now that they had finally connected, he wanted to hold Kate forever, but upon hearing a second knock, he released her from their kiss. Although he hadn't wanted to stop, and he believed that she felt the same, he knew he needed to slow down or he might scare her away. With reluctance, he walked gingerly to the entry and opened the door.

The attendant wheeled in a cart set with fine china settings, a silver teapot and some delicate looking sweets. Noah handed him a five-dollar bill—a lot for him to part with, but he wanted to make a good impression. Then the attendant left.

"Would you like a cuppa?" Noah asked once the door was closed and they were alone again.

Kate nodded as she pushed a stray lock behind her ear.

He poured her a cup of tea then offered it to her. His hand shook ever so slightly, but Kate didn't mention it. She seemed to notice his tentativeness and couldn't help but wonder at their differences—he, so full of life and ambition, but so poor in finances. Her with a career that took her all over the world. He hoped she would see beyond their differences, would recognize how well they fit together, each understanding love and loss.

She sipped her tea and then took a small cookie from the tray. She looked at him straight in the eyes and sighing, she said, "You know, I'm very fond of you . . ."

He winced at those words, as though fearing what would come next. "I'm very fond of you *but* . . ."

Before she could answer, her cell phone played Wagner's *Ride of the Valkyries.* She accepted the call and pressed speaker. Marcy's voice was filled with panic.

"What's up, Marcy?" Kate said.

"Your brother and my daughter are at it again. Megan left a voice message on our home phone, says that she and Josh have waited long enough and that they are eloping tonight."

"Oh!" Kate shouted. "I thought they were going to wait."

Kate took the phone off speaker, apparently so that he couldn't hear the other half of the conversation.

"You tried to call her?" she said, becoming more agitated the longer she talked. "What's wrong with them? I thought they were going to date others and she was going to finish her education. . . . I know he finished school, but she hasn't."

When she finally ended the call, Kate sat with her elbows on her thighs and cradled her head in her hands.

"Kate, what happened?" Noah sat next to her and placed an arm around her shoulders. "Maybe I can help."

"You don't understand." She looked him in the eyes and blurted out, "Megan is my daughter. Oh no, I hadn't meant to tell you in this way," she moaned. "And Josh is my brother."

Noah looked at her, his eyebrows drawn up in confusion.

"Before tonight only three people knew this, Dr. Jamison, Bruce, and Marcy . . . and now I've told you."

"What do you mean that Megan is your daughter?" Noah asked.

During the next two hours, Kate recounted her past to him. Although she had told him long ago that she had retained her memories, she had only told him about her college days and her work.

She clung to him, as though afraid he would leave now that he knew the truth, but instead he sat spellbound.

Bruce had been her husband! Marcy was her physical therapist. She had two children.

He tried to wrap his head around this. How strange the two of them were: her with a body younger than his, but a brain so much older; him, new to physical love, whereas she was experienced—a mother—once a wife; she had a family that she could never claim, he had two; she was so small and pale, he was tall and dark. Were there ever two people so different?

"Kate, do you want me to go?" he asked.

"You hate me now, don't you?" Kate said with a sob.

Noah held her closer. "No. I love you more than life itself. I—I've loved you from the first moment I saw you. I would do anything for you." He made her look into his eyes. "But when I think about what you've told me I realize that my road to surgery was so simple, thanks to you. Yours was so complicated, so . . . shocking."

Kate lifted her head up to him, tilted it to one side and planted a passionate kiss on his lips. Then she pulled him tight to her. "Stay with me tonight. I need you."

It was the hardest thing he had ever done, and to Kate's obvious surprise and confusion, Noah gently pushed her away.

"I'll stay tonight, but only as your friend."

Kate acted crushed.

"We need to talk," he said, looking directly into her eyes. "Then together we'll figure out what to do." He suddenly became more serious. "But, you'll have to marry me if you want me to stay as *more* than a friend."

"Is that a proposal?" she asked.

"Yes. If you'll have me."

"Will I have you?" She threw her arms around him and pressed herself to him. "Of course I will."

Megan looked over at Josh. She felt extreme pride and a deep love for him, and he had promised his undying love to her too. He stood next to her as though nothing could be more natural. And as they both had earlier agreed, Josh wore the same suit that he had worn at the gala almost two years ago and she wore the same dress. It was their way of connecting the beginning of their courtship to their wedding day.

Eloping had seemed like the only way to bridge the gap that his sister, Kate, and Megan's parents had placed on their relationship. Now their family would have to accept the fact that the two of them were bound by holy matrimony.

"Are you ready?" the chaplain asked.

Josh said, "Yes, sir."

Megan nodded.

The ceremony took no more than ten minutes, but there had been music, flowers, witnesses, and a passionate kiss. It was all that Megan needed. She was now Mrs. Megan Craig.

She looked up at Josh. "I may be a modern woman, but I want to take your last name. Just remember, our first child, whether it's a boy or a girl, will be named Lindsay."

"Yes, Mrs. Craig. And we will have the handsomest, prettiest and smartest babies in the world."

After signing the final papers, they waved goodbye to the chaplain and exited the chapel with its gaudy LED-light flashing.

They entered the rented limo and Josh instructed the driver to take them to the Hyatt Hotel where he had reserved the Honeymoon Suite for four nights.

Sneaking away to marry was painful. Megan had always dreamed of a large church wedding with all her friends and family around, but circumstances had crushed that dream. After her family accepted Josh, they could have a church ceremony or maybe on their first anniversary they could renew their vows in a holy place. The Reno chapel hadn't been the first choice for either of them.

But at least it's done.

When they reached the door to their suite, Josh lifted her and carried her over the threshold.

Epilogue

Three Years Later

Noah watched as Kate sat at her antique dressing table, brushing her long hair. He reminisced about the past few years. How lucky he and Kate had been to have had two beautiful ceremonies where they had pledged their love: a top-of-the-line wedding at the Castro Valley United Methodist Church with her family and friends, and two weeks later, a building-packed ceremony at the City Life Church in Melbourne, Australia, with his family and friends.

He smiled to himself as he remembered the look on Donald Jamison's face when Kate asked him to walk her down the aisle in Australia. According to his wife, Inna, it was the first time she had ever seen him cry. He had simply nodded in approval when she had asked him.

Noah walked over to the dressing table and took the brush from Kate's hand and ran the brush through her thick dark hair. "Hurry up girl. Don't take all day getting ready. We are just going to see the doctor."

He couldn't help but wonder at his good fortune. Now he had everything he had ever hoped for: a loving wife, wonderful families, a small but handy apartment not far from his campus, and a new car that could hold a growing family.

Although he was still deep into his studies at UC Davis, what little spare time he had was spent doting over her. She called him, "Kind, thoughtful, romantic, and downright brilliant."

He and Kate glanced up at the picture of Josh and Megan that was taped near the top of the dressing table mirror. They both enjoyed the close ties with them. Their marriage was the perfect solution to all her concerns because they were both now central characters in the lives the Lindsay family and her Craig family. Kate touched her lips and then reached up and fingered the photo.

Now that she was pregnant, Noah and she had agreed that it would be best if she placed her opera career on hold. Some day she would return to the opera, but during the next several months she would save her voice for the church choir and her family. For now, they could live fairly well off the royalties from the sales of her many recordings. That would sustain them until he could enter his practice.

Kate felt movement in her growing belly. She touched it and grinned. Their son would be called Kevin, after Noah's body donor—his name would be Kevin Craig Burnett to be exact. Their little boy would be born within weeks of the date when Megan's and Josh's daughter would be born.

"The appointment at the clinic is just thirty minutes from now. Traffic can hold ya up so we need ta go."

"I just need to slip on my shoes and we can be off," she said. Kate was dressed in a loose-fitting knee-length pink smock and black leggings. She had promised him to only wear flats with good arch support to protect her legs and feet. They were both pleased that her bouts with morning sickness had passed after the third month and now their thoughts centered on preparing for the blessed days—both hers and those of Megan and Josh.

Her mantra had changed. It was no longer "mi, mi, mi," but was "life, life, life."

"Come on, gal. It's getting late." Noah opened the front door and pointed at the car.

"Okay. Just need to take my vitamins," she said as she threw three capsules in her mouth and swallowed them with a gulp of water.

They arrived at the clinic on time. Noah held the door and helped Kate out. "Come on, pretty Mama. Doc's a waiting."

Kate checked in at the front desk. She and Noah took a seat in the waiting room and each picked up a magazine about parenting. They sat transfixed until the nurse called Kate. She weighed in—up two pounds. Not bad. Vital signs all good. The nurse guided them to the examination room. Next, she instructed Kate to disrobe, don the unflattering gown, and then wait for the doctor.

A good fifteen minutes later, Dr. Wong entered. "How's Mr. and Mrs. Burnett today?" he asked.

"I think I'm fine and I hope you tell me the same," Kate said.

Dr. Wong studied her chart for longer than usual before asking her to climb onto the exam table. They heard the doctor hmm and umm several times while examining her.

"Okay, Mrs. Burnett, you can get dressed. I'd like you and Mr. Burnett to meet me in my office when you're ready."

"Is everything alright?" she asked.

"I'm sure there's no problem, but I need to fill you in on some new research."

When the doctor left the office, Kate turned to Noah. "What do you think this is all about?"

"Aye, maybe it's good news, like something new in childbirth techniques," he responded.

They opened the door to the office quietly and all but tiptoed in. Even Noah had told her he felt there was something almost sacred about the Zen-like environment in Wong's office. As they entered they saw that the doctor was reading a chart. He took off his glasses and offered the chairs opposite him.

Doctor Wong cleared his throat. "Please, sit down."

Kate felt a sudden darkening of her spirit. She could tell by his demeanor that whatever he had to share wasn't going to bring joy to her heart.

"I've been doing some research on transplant patients, and I've discovered some facts."

"What is it?" Noah said.

Kate could see that her husband was perched on the edge of his seat, leaning forward. It was obvious to her that he, too, was worried.

"There is a possible condition that develops in transplant patients that could affect the baby. A transplant can leave a patient with dual sets of DNA. Often it is just temporary, but in some cases it is permanent."

"What does that mean?" Kate asked.

"Well, genetic material can be shared within one organism. This is known as Microchimerism. It can occur with blood transfusions and organ and tissue transplantation, and in the case of your baby, it's possible that he could have up to four different sets of DNA since both you and your husband had transplants."

"Could this hurt him?" Noah asked.

"Some scientists have opined that the migration of donor DNA may have long-term, lasting ill-effects."

"Like what?" Kate asked.

"I'll have the receptionist make a copy of this article for you to take home. You and your husband need to study it and make an important decision."

"What do you mean?"

Doctor Wong took in a long breath then said, "It is possible that the incorporation of the foreign DNA could result in physical rearrangements including mutations, deletions . . . and interruptions of the coding sequences and chromosomal breakages." The doctor looked downtrodden as he added, "You need to decide whether you want to take this pregnancy to fruition. It's not too late to abort the pregnancy within the next few weeks."

Kate shook her head wildly. "But we've seen the ultrasound. The baby looks whole and healthy. Just two weeks ago you said everything looked good."

Noah stood up. "Come on, Kate. Let's get out of here. We need to leave."

Noah could see that Kate had tears forming in the corners of her eyes, clearly shaken to her very core.

Kate slowly shook her head and took Noah's hand. "No, Noah. This baby will be just fine. Don't worry." She looked over at the doctor. "There'll be no abortion, Dr. Wong. We'll see you again in two weeks." With that, Kate stood, took her husband's arm, and added, "Let's go see the receptionist and schedule the next appointment." Then she looked back over her shoulder at Dr. Wong. "More than most, we know the value of life, and this little baby," she said as she rubbed her belly, "will smell roses and see starry skies."

Noah placed his arm tightly around Kate's waist. They walked together down the hall to schedule the next consultation.

"You and I, my love, have been pioneers in transplant surgery. We can handle this together," Noah said.

Kate squeezed Noah's hand and rested her head on his shoulder. "No matter what happens, we will get through this," Kate said.

Noah looked down at the love of his life. He knew that she was with him one hundred percent. As long as he had that, their love could handle whatever life sent their way.

Kate felt her baby kick and put Noah's hand on her stomach. He smiled. LIFE!

THE END

Discussion Questions

1. Will Kate ever tell Megan and Mark that she has their late mother's brain and memories, or will she keep this secret to her grave?

2. Do you think that the day will come when brain transplants will be possible? Would such a procedure be seen as man trying to play God?

3. How well or poorly did Bruce and Marcy handle the return of Kate/Liz?

4. With which character, if any, were you able to identify?

5. Will Kate return to the stage, and if so, what effect might it have on her family and her relationships?

6. Months after Noah got his donor body, he had trouble texting because his hands were so much bigger than those he was accustomed to. How difficult might it be to adjust to a body that is wholly different from the one in which you were born?

7. In your opinion, is the on-the-road theater and opera life lonely, or would the celebrations and fans fulfill one's social needs?

Acknowledgments

There may not be enough space to thank all my friends and relatives who helped review and comment on *Discovering Kate* during its development. I especially must thank my step-daughter, Carol Craig, for reviewing, editing, and helping me meet deadlines. I would be remiss not to mention the patience and long nights that my husband, Howard, endured as I sat in hidden for hours in my tiny office. Thank you to Karen Guardagno, Howard's caregiver, who not only kept him entertained when I was busy typing, but read the first draft and gave me new insights that changed the direction of the novel. A special thanks goes to my book clubs that have kept after me to give "Kate" a longer life.

About the Author

Dixie Owens is an alumnus of the University of Southern California and holds a "Women in Management" certificate from USC's post-graduate school of business. She enjoyed a long career with the California Employment Development Department (EDD) and retired as Deputy Director of Public Affairs.

After retirement, with long-time friend Gloria Powers, she volunteered to co-instruct classes at Mustard Seed, a school for homeless youth. After she and her husband, Howard, relocated to Oregon, she served as volunteer with the local food bank. She and her spouse are currently members of the Grants Pass chapter of Lions International, an all-volunteer organization that raises funds to provide glasses and hearing aids for the needy.

She loves to serve her community, write, read, swim, grand-parent, and sing. She currently sings with her church's choir and with In Accord, a ten-woman a capella group that performs for civic events and retirement homes.

Dixie and her husband have a shared family of seven children (and their respective spouses), fifteen grandchildren, and eight great-grandchildren. It's Dixie's job to keep track of birthdays, weddings, graduations, and other such important events.

Her first novel, *Becoming Kate*, debuted at the local library and has been a favorite of book clubs both locally and abroad. She also has self-published a children's picture book, *The Curious Kitten*. The artwork was skillfully done by one of her song-mates, Judy Strode.

Discovering Kate was written as a stand-alone novel, but fans who loved *Becoming Kate* will view it as a long-awaited sequel.

Scan to visit

www.dixieowens.com